WHAT'S A HOUSEKEEPER TO DO?

WHAT'S A HOUSEKEEPER TO DO?

BY

JENNIE ADAMS

First published in Great Britain 2010
Large Print edition 2010
Harlequin Mills & Boon Limited,
Eton House, 18-24 Paradise Road,
Richmond, Surrey TW9 1SR

© Jennifer Ann Ryan 2010

ISBN: 978 0 263 21250 1

Harlequin Mills & Boon policy is to use papers that are
natural, renewable and recyclable products and made
from wood grown in sustainable forests. The logging and
manufacturing process conform to the legal environmental
regulations of the country of origin.

Printed and bound in Great Britain
by CPI Antony Rowe, Chippenham, Wiltshire

For the girls in my bunker.
For cheeky lunch-time topics and midnight IMs.
For the Toby addiction (yes, you L),
for the Rwoooarhhh! (yes, you C).
For talking me down on the phone (yes, you V).
For hugs in person and hugs long distance.
For being my cheer squad.
For sharing the path with me with grace.
For understanding about the boots.
For my editor Joanne Grant,
and my senior editor Kim Young.
I am blessed. Thank you.
For my precious ones, and for you.

CHAPTER ONE

'I REALISE it's a little unusual, conducting this kind of business in the middle of a lake.' Cameron Travers' mouth turned up with a hint of self-directed humour before he shrugged broad shoulders in the misty Adelaide morning air. 'When I started wondering about this scene idea, and I knew I'd need a second pair of hands to test it out, I decided to combine our interview with some research. I hope you don't mind too much.'

'It's a nice setting for a job interview, Mr Travers, even if it is unusual. I'm more than happy to oblige.' If the man needed to row a boat around a lake at dawn to research for his crime-thriller writing, then Lally Douglas could work with that. She offered what she hoped appeared to be a completely relaxed smile because, yes, she did have a little bout of nerves going on. After all, she'd never had a 'real' job-interview before, let alone with a millionaire property-developer and world-famous crime-thriller author!

Cameron's attractive mouth curved. 'I appreciate your willing attitude. I could really do with some help for a while with the basics of day to day life so I can focus my energy on the property development I'm undertaking here in Adelaide, and to crack the challenges I'm having with writing my current book.'

The words somehow let her in. His smile let her in further. How could a simple, wry grin all but stop a girl's breath? Lally searched for the answer in deep-green eyes fringed with curly black lashes, in a lean face that was all interesting angles and planes in the early-morning light. In the charming sense of welcome and acceptance that seemed to radiate from him.

She'd sensed he was a nice man when they'd spoken on the phone to arrange this interview. They'd both approached a local job-agency and got an almost immediate match. And now again when they met up here in this leafy Adelaide suburban park to conduct his research experiment, and her job interview.

He was quiet, thoughtful even, and, from the depths Lally discerned in his eyes, he seemed to be a man who kept his share of things to himself. He also had a lovely way of making others feel somehow welcomed by him. 'I'd love to be able to help you so you could concentrate more of your efforts on your work.'

'Having someone to handle housekeeping and some general secretarial work for me—very basic stuff—will free up enough of my time so I can really do that.' Cameron Travers continued to row their small boat out towards the middle of the lake.

Not with muscle-bound arms, Lally. You're not even noticing the muscles in his arms. You're focused on this interview.

Eight weeks of employment as his temporary housekeeper with a little secretarial work thrown in as and when needed: that was what was on offer if she landed the job. Such a period of time in her life would be a mere blip, really.

'Did the agency explain what I'd want from

you?' Cameron asked the question as he rowed. 'I gave them a list of specifics when I lodged my request.'

'I'd have the option of living in or arriving each morning. I'd cook, clean, take phone messages, maybe do a little clerical work, and generally keep things in order for you.'

Lally had no trouble parroting the work conditions. And, feeling that openness was the best policy from the start, she said, 'I would prefer to live in. It would be cheaper than staying with Mum and Dad and travelling across the city each day to get to work.' Well, if she had to take a job outside the family, the least she could do was choose something she felt would be interesting and make herself comfortable in it.

'You have a good understanding of my requirements. I've always done everything for myself.' His brows drew together. 'But time is ticking away. My agent is getting twitchy. I need to hone my focus on the book and the property development and nothing else. I'm sure taking this step will be all I need to get past the writer's block that's been plaguing me.'

Lally didn't know how long it took to write a top-selling novel in a crime-thriller series, but she imagined it would be quite stressful not to be able to get the story moving while the days rushed by towards a deadline.

And, for Lally, she needed to work to put some money in the coffers. When the job ended she would dig back into her usual place among her relatives and continue to look after them through a variety of gainful employment opportunities.

For their sake. Lally worked for their sake. And it didn't mean there was anything wrong just because she'd been obliged to get out into the real workforce at this time either. No one in the entire mix-and-match brood happened to need her just at the moment. That was all.

Lally tipped her chin up into the air, drew a deep breath and forced her attention to their surroundings; South Australia in November. It was cool and misty over the lake this morning, but that was only because the park was shaded, leafy, the lake substantial and the hour still early. Later it would get quite warm.

'It is certainly mood-inducing weather,' Lally said. 'For this kind of research.'

'Yes, and the burst of rain last night has resulted in a nice mist effect here this morning.' He glanced about them.

Lally was too interested in the man, not the scenery. She admitted this, though she rather wished she hadn't noticed him quite so particularly. She usually worked very hard to avoid noticing men. She'd been there and made a mess of it. She still carried the guilt of the fallout. What had happened had been so awful—

Lally pushed the thoughts away and turned her attention to the dip of the oars through the water, turned her attention back to Cameron Travers, which was where it needed to be. Just not with quite so much consciousness of him as a man. She trailed her fingers through the water for a moment and quickly withdrew them.

'You said on the phone yesterday that you have plenty of experience in housekeeping?' The corners of Cameron's eyes crinkled as he studied her.

Lally nodded. 'I've worked in a housekeeping

role more than once. I'm a confident cook, and I know how to efficiently organise my time and my surroundings. I'm a quick learner, and used to being thrown in the deep end to deal with an array of tasks. I see new challenges as fun.'

'That sounds like what I need.' His voice held approval, and for some silly reason her heart pattered once again as she registered this fact.

'I hope so.' Lally glanced away and blabbed out the first thing that came to her mind. 'Well, it may be November, but trailing my fingers through that water made it clear it's still quite chilly. I wouldn't want to fall in.'

'Or dip your hand into water that might be hiding a submerged crocodile.' Cameron eased back on the oars a little. 'Wrong end of Australia for that, of course.'

'I've spent time in the Northern Territory and the Torres Strait islands. I have relatives up that way, on my mother's side of the family, but I've never seen a crocodile close up.' Lally suppressed a shudder. 'I don't want to.'

Lally didn't want to fall into awareness of her potential new boss, either—not that she was comparing him to a dangerous crocodile. And not that she was falling into awareness.

Cameron gave a thoughtful look as he continued to ply the oars until they reached the centre of the lake. Once there, he let the boat drift. 'It looks quite deep out here. I suspect the water would stay cold even in mid-summer.'

In keeping with the cool of the morning, he wore a cream sweater and blue jeans. The casual clothes accentuated his musculature and highlighted the green of his eyes.

Lally glanced at her own clothing of tan trousers and black turtleneck top. She needed to take a leaf out of her dress-mode book and be sensible about this interview, instead of being distracted by the instigator of it. She drew a steadying breath and gestured to the package in the bottom of the boat. 'You said we'd be tossing that overboard?'

He'd told her that much about his morning's mission when they'd met where the boat had been moored, at a very small-scale jetty at the edge of the lake.

'Yes. It's only a bundle of sand in a bio-friendly wrapping. I'll be using my imagination for the rest.' His gaze narrowed as he took careful note of their surroundings. 'I need to get the combination of atmosphere and mechanics properly balanced in my mind. How much of a splash would there be? How much sound? How far out would the water ripple? The dumping would need to build tension without the reader figuring out what's going on, so I'm after atmosphere as well.'

'Ooh. You could throw a body over.' Lally paused to think. 'Well, no, the sand isn't heavy enough for that. What are you throwing in the story—a weapon? Part of a body?'

'Do I detect a hint of blood-thirsty imagination there?' He laughed, perhaps at the caught-out expression that must have crossed her face.

'Oh, no. Well, I guess maybe I was being blood-thirsty…a little.' Lally drew a breath and returned his smile. 'You must have a lot of fun writing your stories.'

'Usually I do.' His gaze stilled on her mouth and he appeared arrested for a very brief moment before he blinked. Whatever expression she'd glimpsed in his eyes disappeared.

'If you take me on as your housekeeper, I'll do everything I can to help you.' When she'd applied for this job Lally had only had two criteria in her mind: it had to be temporary, and she had to feel she could do the required work. Now she realised this truly could be interesting as well, even perhaps a little exciting; there was also plenty of room for a sense of achievement and to know that she had truly helped someone.

She might only be the housekeeper, but she'd be housekeeping for a crime writer on a deadline!

If it occurred to Lally that she had been a little short on excitement for a while, she immediately pushed that thought aside.

Lally shifted on her bench seat and quickly stilled the motion. She didn't want to rock the boat—literally. 'I haven't read anything suspenseful for a while. I usually save that for watching movies, but a good crime novel, curled up on a sofa…' She drew a breath. 'I'll try not to badger you with questions while you're plotting and writing. Well, that is, if you end up employing me.'

'I doubt it would bother me if you asked questions.' He smiled. 'Provided they don't start or end with the words "How many pages have you written today?"'

'I think I could manage not to ask that.' That would be like her mum painting, or Auntie Edie working with her pottery, and Lally demanding an account of the time they'd spent.

Lally cast another glance at Cameron Travers. He shared her dark hair, though his was short and didn't grow in waves, unlike her own corkscrew curls that flowed halfway down her back.

He had lightly tanned skin, and 'come lose yourself in me' eyes; now that she looked closely she saw very permanent-looking smudges beneath those beautiful eyes.

So, the man had a flaw in his appeal. He wasn't totally stunning and irresistible to look at.

If you could call looking weary a flaw. 'Will I be helping you to get more rest?' That hadn't exactly come out as she'd intended. 'That is, I don't mean to suggest I'll be boring you to sleep at the dinner table or something.' He probably had a girlfriend to fuss over him anyway. Or maybe one tucked in every port, just like Sam had.

Well, Sam had had a wife.

And Lally.

She was not going there.

Sam was a topic Lally rarely allowed to climb all the way to the surface of her thoughts. It annoyed her that it had happened now—twice, really, if she counted that earlier memory of the mess she'd made of her life, and several others in the process.

Lally stiffened her spine and firmed her full lips into what she hoped was a very business-like expression. 'I'll help you in any way that I can. It's just that you look a bit exhausted. That's why I asked the question.'

'Your help would allow me to focus my energy where I need to.' His gaze searched hers. 'That would be as good as helping me to get more rest. I don't sleep much.

'Now, are you ready to toss the sand-bundle overboard for me? It's quite a few kilos in weight. I do need a woman to throw it, as the "passenger" in the boat, but I hadn't stopped to think...' He hesitated and his gaze took in Lally's slender frame.

'I can manage it.' Lally flicked her hair over her shoulder where it wouldn't get in her way.

She might be slender but she was five-foot-seven inches in height and she had plenty of strength. If she could lift her nieces, nephews and little cousins of various sizes and ages, she could toss a packet of sand. 'Any time you're ready. Shall I stand and drop it like a bomb—hurl it from a sitting position? Do you want a plop or a splash, water spraying back into the boat?'

'Hurling would be fine, thank you. Preferably far enough out that we don't get drenched in the process.' Did Cameron's lips go from a twitch to a half-concealed grin? 'I think you should be able to throw the packet from a standing position, if we're careful. I do want to try that.'

He clasped her hand to help her come upright, and there went her resolve not to notice him in the slide of warm, dry skin over her palm, in the clasp of strong fingers curled around her hand.

Lally braced her feet and gave a slight cough. 'I'm, eh, I'm fine now, thanks. I have my balance. You can let go.'

He did so and she stifled a reaction that felt as

much like disappointment as relief. It was neither, of course, because she wasn't fazed one way or the other by his touch.

Really, how could the clasp of a hand for a couple of seconds, a down-bent gaze as he helped her up, a curve of a male cheek and the view of a dark-haired head, make her heart beat faster?

How could his gaze looking right into her eyes, and his expression focusing with utter totality on her for one brief blink in time, make her feel attractive to him, for Pete's sake?

Trust me, Lally, you are not necessary to his very ability to breathe. You're looking like a solid possibility as a temporary employee, maybe, but the rest?

'Ready?' Cameron met her gaze with raised brows.

Lally uttered, 'Yes.'

He put the packet into her hands. It was heavy, but she invested all her effort into tossing it.

It landed several feet away with a satisfying splash and she eased back into her seat while Cameron's eyes narrowed. He mentally cata-logued the impact—the upward splash of water droplets, water rippling out, the way the mist seemed to swallow everything just moments after it happened.

Lally watched Cameron, then realised what she was doing and abruptly looked away.

'Thank you. At least I know now that with two in the boat, even if he's otherwise occupied, she can toss the package over without drawing too much attention.' He stopped and smiled. 'Now that we've taken care of my research, tell me about your previous work-experience.' Cameron's words drew her gaze back to his face.

And put everything back in to perspective as an interview, which was of course exactly what Lally wanted.

'You don't need to make notes?' Well, obviously he didn't, or he would be doing so. She waved away the silly question. 'I've worked for the past six years for my extended family, doing all kinds of things: housekeeping, bookkeeping and cooking. I've been a waitress at my father's restaurant, *Due per*. It's small, but the place is always packed with diners.

'I've worked at my uncle's fresh-produce store,

and another relative's fishing-tackle shop. My mother, several of her sisters and a couple of brothers are all Aboriginal and Torres Strait artists of one description or another. I've helped them at times, too, plus I've done nanny duties for my three sisters, and my brother and his wife.'

Lally drew a breath. 'I've travelled with Mum on painting expeditions. Anything the family's needed from me, I've done.' Except she had avoided Mum and Auntie Edie's attempts to get her to paint. Lally somehow hadn't felt ready for that, but that wasn't the point.

She fished in the deep orange, crushed-velour shoulder-bag she'd tucked beneath her seat and pulled out her references. Lally fingered the three-inch thick wad of assorted papers. 'I gave the employment agency three, but these are the rest. I have everything here that you might want to see in relation to my work experience.'

A hint of warmth crept into Lally's high cheeks. 'I probably didn't need to bring all of them.' But how could she have cut it down to just a few, chosen just some of them over the others?

'Better too many than not enough. May I see?'

He held out one lean hand and Lally placed the papers into it.

Their fingers brushed as they made the exchange. One part of her wanted to prolong the contact, another worried that he'd know the impact his touch had on her. The same thing had happened when he'd helped her into the boat this morning.

Cameron flicked through the pages, stopping here and there to read right through. Aunt Judith had written her reference on an indigenous-art letterhead and added a postscript: *Latitia needs to pursue art in her personal time before she gets a lot older.* At least Aunt Judith hadn't labelled the reference with 'B-'. That was what Lally got for having an aunt who'd been a school-teacher before she left work to paint full-time.

Cameron's mouth definitely quirked at one corner as he read Aunt Judith's admonishment.

Her uncle's reference was on a fruit-shop order form. Well, it was the content that counted.

'I don't know how you manage with so many relatives.' The concept seemed utterly alien to Cameron.

'Is your family…?' *Small? Non-existent?* Lally cut off the question; not her business, not her place to ask.

And just because she needed her family the way she did didn't mean everyone felt like that.

'There's only ever been my mother.' His gaze lifted to her face and he gave her a thoughtful look. He cleared his throat and returned his attention to the references. As his expression eased into repose, the sense of weariness about him returned.

How did he survive in life with only one relative? His expression had been hard to read when he'd mentioned his mother. Lally imagined they must be extremely close.

'I'm more than happy with the references.' Cameron said this decisively as he watched a grey-teal duck glide across the water beside them. 'Do you have computer skills?'

'I can type at about fifty words a minute in a basic word-processing programme, and I've spent plenty of time on the Internet.' Lally would do her best. She always gave one-hundred-and-fifty percent. 'You said on the phone that you're refurbishing the old Keisling building. I looked it up on Google. The place looks quite large; it must be a substantial project to undertake.'

Adelaide had a lot of old buildings. Lally loved the atmosphere of the city; it combined a big, flat sprawliness with all mod cons.

'The Keisling building was initially a huge home. I'll be converting it to apartments.' He nodded. 'Once the work is done, I'll either sell it or put tenants in.'

'There are a lot of old buildings in Adelaide that I haven't seen.' Lally made the comment as he began to row them back towards shore. 'I've seen a reasonable amount of Australia generally, though.' She paused as she realised the interview appeared to be over. 'Am I rambling?'

'Slightly, but I don't mind. You have a soothing voice.' Cameron continued to row. 'I've travelled a lot myself. Sydney is where I keep a permanent apartment, and I'm in the same boat with that.' He glanced at the oars in his hands and humour warmed his eyes. 'I know a lot of Australia, but there are parts of Sydney that I don't know at all. There's a tendency to stick to what you need to know on local turf sometimes, isn't there?'

'Indeed there is.' Now Lally could add 'empathy' and 'able to laugh at himself' to his list of attributes. Employer's attributes. 'Do you often travel and incorporate your writing research or settings with your property-development projects?'

'Yes. I work long hours and need to keep occupied, so I actively seek ways to keep my mind fresh and to keep busy.' A slight sound that could have been a sigh escaped him before he returned his attention to his rowing. 'Property development came first for me. I got into that straight out of school, and was fortunate enough to make money and be able to expand and make a strong, successful business of it. When I needed more to keep me occupied, I hit on the idea of writing a book. I mostly started that for my own amusement because I enjoyed reading. I was quite surprised when my first book was picked up by an agent, and from there a publisher. Making a second career out of writing was an unexpected bonus.'

And now he entertained and fascinated readers around the world.

I'm not fascinated by him, Lally told herself.

But her other side wanted to know why she couldn't be a little fascinated within reason, provided the fascination was focused on his work. 'And you became a famous author.'

'An author with a looming deadline and an unwelcome bout of writer's block.' Cameron brushed off her reference to his fame.

But he was famous. His series had gained a lot of popularity over the past few years. He had become at least somewhat a household name.

Cameron seemed to hesitate before he went on. 'Usually I'd thrive on my deadlines, but lately? There's the development of this property to get in motion, the rest of the business to keep an eye on via remote control and I'm more tired than usual—maybe because I've been pushing harder with the writing, trying to get somewhere with it.'

He didn't just want an assistant, he *needed* one.

The knowledge went straight to the part of Lally that had given herself to her family so exclusively for the past six years. The part that yes, had felt just a little threatened when they hadn't needed her at the end of her last job. Even her sisters had said no to child minding, and they were always asking if Lally could find blocks of time for that.

'Oh, no thanks, Lally. I've put them all into after-school care and a sports programme for the next few months.'

'Actually, Ray's parents are going to have the girls after school for a while.'

And so it had gone on.

Who'd heard of Douglas children going to after-school care? The family did that! And Ray's parents never had them.

It had felt like a conspiracy, but that thought was silly. Lally shoved it aside accordingly.

'You need to be looked after a little, to have someone to take the stress off you so you can focus on what you most need to get done.' Lally could care for this man for two months, and then she would go back to where she wanted and needed to be—to the heart of the family who had all been there for her through thick and thin. 'I'll be the best housekeeper and assistant I possibly can, Mr Travers, if you choose to employ me.'

Cameron eased the boat in towards the make-shift dock. 'I do want to employ you.' He named a generous salary. 'We'll need to figure out what days you'll be having off, that sort of thing.'

'I have the job? Oh, thank you!' The wash of happiness Lally experienced had to be relief that she would be financially secure for the next two months, she decided. Her family would have helped her out, of course, they'd all offered that. But she couldn't accept that kind of support and then just sit around and twiddle her thumbs.

So this was good. Very good. 'Thank you, Mr Travers. I'll do everything I can to be a valuable employee to you.'

For some reason he looked quite taken aback for a moment. Cameron let the small craft bump into the dock. 'How soon can you start?'

'Later today, or first thing tomorrow. Which would suit you best?' Lally said—judiciously, she hoped, though excitement was bubbling all through her.

'Let's go with first thing tomorrow.' Cameron

left the boat with an agility that made it look easy. He extended his hand and offered a smile that seemed to wash right through her. 'It will be nice to have someone else in charge of some of these things while I try…'

He didn't complete the sentence, but Lally assured herself that that was not because he was distracted by the touch of her hand in his.

More likely he had to focus on not letting her plop into the water like that packet of sand, because she wasn't paying as much attention to proceedings as she should have been as she wobbled her way out of the boat and onto the dock.

Pay attention, Lally, to getting your feet on solid ground—or planks as the case may be— not to the feel of warm skin against your hand!

'Um, thank you.' Lally detached her hand from where it had somehow managed to wrap very securely around his. She could feel the pink tingeing her cheeks again; yes, it was possible to *feel* pink.

'You were about to say, while you try…?'

'To manage two key areas of my life so they

both get, and stay, under control.' Cameron pushed his hands into the pockets of his trousers.

He appeared quite unaware of the way that the action shifted the cream jumper across his chest so Lally could enjoy an unimpeded view of the movement of the muscles that ran beneath the layer of cloth.

She was not noticing!

To make up for her consciousness, Lally gifted Cameron Travers with a full-wattage, 'thank you for employing me' smile. 'Your property work and your writing. I understand. So, seven tomorrow morning at your development site, bags packed and ready to leap straight in to whatever is on your agenda for the day? Me, not the bags, I mean.'

Cameron blinked once, and the dark green of his eyes darkened further. 'Yes. That will be fine. We'll eat breakfast while I give you a list of duties to start you off.'

'Excellent.' Lally considered shaking his hand again, and rejected the idea.

Better to keep her hands to herself. Instead, she tucked a long brown curl behind her ear and turned towards the exit of the park. 'I'll see you tomorrow, Mr Travers.'

'Cam,' he offered mildly, and took her elbow in a gentle grip. 'Cameron, if you really must. I'll walk you back to your car.'

'And I'm Latitia. Well, you'd have seen that on my job application and some of the references. But I prefer Lally. Um, will your boat be safe?' Lally's words ran together in a breathless rush.

'I hired the boat. The owner should be along to collect it soon.' Cameron didn't seem worried one way or the other.

He could probably simply buy a replacement. The man no doubt had the money to do that if he wanted.

Lally hot-footed it at his side to the exit as quickly as she could, where she immediately made her way to her elderly, fuel-inefficient station wagon, and bade him an equally swift farewell. The car seated six people, and that was important when a girl had a really big family. She needed to regroup and get her thoughts sorted between now and tomorrow, so she could approach this new work from the right perspective. From a completely efficient, professionally detached, businesslike perspective.

'See you tomorrow.' He turned to walk towards his own car, parked some distance beyond them.

The last thing Lally saw as she drove away was Cameron getting into a sky-blue convertible and putting the top down.

Her final thought was of how much she would love a drive through the countryside in that vehicle with him.

Even if it would only fit the two of them.

Not that she was thinking of them as 'two'.

That would be just plain silly, and dangerous into the bargain.

Lally hadn't protected her emotions and avoided men for the past six years to now get herself into trouble again in that respect!

CHAPTER TWO

'HERE I am, suitcases in tow as promised.' Lally spoke the words in a tone that was determinedly cheerful and didn't quite cover a hint of nerves.

She pulled the suitcases in question behind her along the courtyard pathway. 'I have more things in my car, but I can get those later. I pretty much take my whole world with me to every new job among the family; it's a habit I've formed over the years. I like to surround myself with my belongings. That way I can feel at "home" wherever I am. I'm sure I'll feel at home here, too, once I've settled in.'

Perhaps she'd formed the habit of chattering sometimes to try to hide things such as nerves.

Cam felt an odd need, that seemed to start in the middle of his chest, to reassure her and set her at her ease. He rose from where he'd been seated at the outdoor dining-table, and started towards her.

'I take a few regular things along when I travel.' Those things were mostly to do with both aspects of his work commitments: laptops, business files, his coffee machine and research materials for his writing. The coffee machine was definitely work related! 'Let me help you with that lot; your load looks ten times heavier than you. And I'm looking forward to you getting settled here too.'

It was ages since he'd spent any significant amount of time in close company with a woman. The last effort had been a disaster, but this was different, a working relationship. Cam wanted his housekeeper to feel welcome and comfortable.

She drew in a deep breath and let it out slowly, and he watched much of the tension ease out of her.

Lally Douglas was a beautiful woman. It would be a very novel experience for him, to have a woman living in as his housekeeper, and to have this woman specifically. He'd anticipated someone older, perhaps in semi-retirement.

Maybe he would learn some things through

contact with Lally Douglas that would help him to pin down the quirks and foibles of the female character for his book.

He did wonder why his new housekeeper carried that edge of reserve that seemed contrary to the vibrancy of her imagination, and the sparkle in her deep-brown eyes when something interested her. Cam put this curiosity down to his writer's mind, and studied Lally for a moment from beneath lowered lashes.

She was a slender girl with skin the colour of milky coffee, and curly almost-black hair; she had thick lashes, high cheekbones and a heart-melting smile that revealed perfect white teeth when it broke over her face. Today she wore a tan skirt that reached to her knees, sandals with a low heel, a simple white blouse and a light camel-coloured cardigan thrown over her shoulders.

'I can manage the suitcases.' Lally gestured behind her. 'As you can see, they stack, and the whole lot is on wheels.'

'Yes, I can see.' But he took the handle from her anyway. Their hands brushed and he tried, really tried, not to notice the smoothness of her skin or the long, slender fingers with perfectly trimmed, unadorned nails. Cam wanted to stroke that soft skin, wrap those fingers in his.

And do what? Bring her hand to his lips and kiss her fingertips? *Not happening, Travers.* He'd had this same reaction to her yesterday, and had done his utmost then to stifle it. Mixing business with awareness to a woman really wasn't a smart idea.

Cam didn't have time to worry about an attraction anyway right now. He saved that for when he felt like socialising, and chose companions who were not looking for a long-term involvement. Past experiences in his life hadn't exactly helped him to trust in the concept of women in deeper, personal relationships, between the way his mother had raised him and the one relationship he'd tried to build in his early twenties that had failed abysmally.

Cam towed the load of suitcases to the doorway of the complex's large apartment and pushed them inside before he turned back to Lally.

She had dropped her hand to her side almost awkwardly. Now she gave a small smile. 'Thank you for that.'

'You're welcome.' He gestured behind him. 'That's the apartment we'll share while you're with me. It's the only one in the building that's been kept in half-decent order and fully furnished, as caretakers have come and gone prior to my purchase of the place. I've claimed one of the bedrooms for office space, but there are two more, as well as all the other necessary amenities.'

'That will be fine. Dad checked with the agency and confirmed your character references.' She bit her lip.

'It's best to feel certain that you're safe.' Cam led the way to the outdoor-dining setting and indicated she should take her seat. It was a large table, with half a dozen wrought-iron chairs padded with cushions facing each other around it. Lally and Cam sat at one end.

'Thank you; I appreciate that you understand.' Lally's gaze went to the covered food-dishes and settled on the silver coffee-pot. 'If all that's as good as it smells, I think I'm being very spoiled on my first morning at work.'

Cam shrugged, though her words had pleased

him. 'It took less than half an hour to put together. I cooked while I tried to brainstorm some more ideas for my story.' 'Tried' being the operative word.

'I'll make sure I have a good breakfast ready for you each morning from now on.' As Lally spoke the words, the noise level at the far end of the site increased as two of the workers began to throw tiles off the roof into a steel transport-bin below.

Lally tipped her head to one side and her big, brown eyes filled with good-natured awareness. 'Has the noise been interfering with your writing?'

'No. I can usually work through any amount of noise.' He wished he *could* blame his lack of productivity on that. Cam didn't know what to blame it on, or how to fix it, other than sticking at the writing until he got a breakthrough with this tricky character, and using Lally's help to allow him to really hone his focus on that. 'But they only actually started the work this morning. I've been here less than a week myself, and most of that time's been spent organising a work crew, working with the site boss to get our orders in for materials, that sort of thing.'

Cam liked a good work challenge. He just wasn't enjoying it quite as much as usual this time, thanks to his problems with the book. He'd always managed both aspects of his life—the property development and the writing—and kept both in order. He didn't like feeling out of control at one end of the spectrum.

'It's good that noise isn't a problem to you.' Lally glanced around her, taking in the large pool that looked more like a duck pond at the moment. 'Oh, look at the swimming pool. It's a nice shape, isn't it? A kind of curvy-edged, squished-in-the-middle rectangle. Very mellow.' Her gaze moved around the large courtyard area, and encompassed the building that surrounded it in a U-shape on three sides, before returning to meet his eyes.

'I can see why you wanted this place. It will be wonderful when the work is done.' An expression that seemed to combine interest in her new job and a measure of banked-down hurt came over her face. 'At least I'll have plenty to do here while my family don't need me.' She drew a breath.

'Ah—your family?'

'I'll be back in the thick of it with them straight after this.' She rushed the words out as though maybe she needed to do so, to fully believe in them herself. 'I help out in all sorts of ways.'

'I'm lucky to have you to look after me for a while.' It was true. His body was exhausted, pushed by even more hard work beyond the usual state of tolerable weariness induced by him being an insomniac-workaholic. 'It'll be nice to have someone to take care of some of the very ordinary everyday tasks.'

Heaven knew, he could afford to pay for the help; he'd just never sought it before. Doing the cooking and cleaning for himself burned up time, and time was something he usually had oodles of on his hands. He still had lots of time, but, thanks to a female character who simply refused to come to life on the page for him, that time wasn't productive enough.

Cam lifted the coffee pot, glanced at the cup in front of Lally and raised his eyebrows in a silent question.

'Yes please.' The colour of her eyes changed

from dark brown to clear sherry and a dimple broke out in her cheek. 'I'm ready for my first dose of caffeine for the day.'

They sipped in silence for a moment. Cam let the rich brew hit the back of his throat and give his body a boost. He'd tried leaving coffee out of his diet for a while, hoping it might have a positive impact on his sleep issues, but it hadn't made any difference.

Lally laced her fingers together in front of her on the table and looked about her again. 'This property would make a great base for a character in your book.'

She cast a sheepish glance his way. 'I bought the first book in your series yesterday after our interview. It said in the back that you sometimes use your development projects as settings for your stories.'

'I hope you're enjoying the read.' It made Cam happy to know he was providing entertainment for readers, but Lally had said she didn't usually read crime novels. 'My kind of books aren't to everyone's taste.'

Lally said earnestly, 'Oh, I finished it! I was

on the edge of my seat the whole time. I'm looking forward to reading the rest of the books in the series so far. The only thing that could have made the story better would have been a love interest for your hero.' She clapped a hand over her mouth. 'I'm so sorry. What would I know about it?'

Cam gave a wry grimace. 'The need for a love interest is an opinion shared by my editor and agent. I'm quite prepared to add her in, but I'm having trouble cracking her characterisation.

'Let's eat, anyway.' Cam lifted the covers off the hot food and invited her to help herself. He'd prepared bacon, eggs, sausages and grilled tomatoes, and had added fresh bread-rolls from the small bakery two blocks away. 'I hope there's something here that's to your taste, but if not I have cereal, fruit and yoghurt inside as well.'

'This will be fine. Thank you.' She helped herself to an egg, two grilled tomatoes and a warmed bread roll. 'I'm truly sorry for what I said about your book. It's none of my business.' Lally still looked stricken. 'I shouldn't have told you that I wished there was a female counter-part in that book.'

Cam said gently, 'It's all right. My ego can take some constructive criticism of my work. Who knows? I might bounce some of my ideas off you. In fact, I'll almost certainly ask you to help with research, as you know your way around a computer and the Internet.' That was a bonus Cam hadn't expected to get in his temporary housekeeper.

'Ooh. Helping will be fun.' Lally's eyes gleamed. 'I can look up all sorts of interesting things for you.'

Cam smiled. 'Perhaps I should just be grateful that my editor and agent waited until my sixth book to talk to me about the need to include this new character.'

'Yes. You escaped it until now.' Her grin started in the depths of chocolate eyes, crinkled the skin at their corners and spread across her lips like sunshine.

Teasing; she was teasing him.

And Cam was enjoying being teased. A corresponding smile spread across his face and they stared at each other; the atmosphere changed and suddenly he was looking deep into her eyes and the humour was gone. His hand lifted towards her.

He dropped it back to his side. They broke eye contact at the same time.

Cam reminded himself that this awareness he felt towards her, and that she perhaps felt towards him, wasn't a good thing. Cam lived a chronically busy lifestyle. It had been that way for years. He pushed himself to survive, survived to push himself more. By doing both, he filled the endless hours in which he could never manage to sleep properly.

There was no breaking that cycle. He had to live with it. It was the only way he could live. It certainly wasn't a cycle that lent itself to him getting into any kind of meaningful relationship with a woman. He'd proved that fact in the past.

Yet, you're thirty-two now. What if you get hit with one of those biological urges and need to settle down, produce children or something?

Like his mother had produced and settled. Well, she'd produced.

Cam shoved the conjecture aside. It was quite pointless.

Lally took another sip of coffee and looked at him over the rim of the cup. 'This is very nice. Thank you. I have to admit, I hang out for my first dose of coffee each morning.' She gestured towards the far side of the building. 'The work crew seem to know what they're doing. If they keep on at that cracking pace, the work will be done quickly.'

'That's my goal.' Cam glanced towards the crew and then let his gaze trail slowly back over the courtyard area; a small frown formed between his brows. 'I'm not quite sure what to do out here. It needs something.' He didn't know what; surely getting the place organised into apartments was enough anyway?

He was only going to rent or sell them, so what did it matter if he thought the courtyard lacked soul? 'I want to have the pool converted so it's heated for year-round use. The courtyard and surrounding gardens need to be brought up to scratch as well.'

'The place will be a hive of activity for the next while.'

They ate in silence for a few moments. Cam watched Lally's delicate movements, observed the straightness of her back in the wrought-iron chair.

Her fingers were lovely. If Cam had to create a female love-interest for his book, she would have hands like Lally's, he decided. They'd look good wrapped around a gun, a champagne glass or an assassin's throat while his heroine resisted the threat with all her worth, or the woman could even be an assassin.

Cam had lots of ideas. He just couldn't seem to hone them into something coherent. He cleared his throat. 'The duties list…'

'Do you have a written list for me?' Lally asked her question at the same time.

They stopped and each took a sip of their coffee. Lally drew a breath that lifted her small breasts beneath the cowl-neck top. Her hair was loose about her shoulders, as it had been yesterday.

Her top was sleeveless, and Cam wanted to stroke his fingers over the soft smoothness of her skin. She had strength in those slender arms, despite her small size. So much for deciding he wasn't going to notice her appeal.

While Lally nibbled on a bite of tomato, Cam fished a piece of paper from his shirt pocket. 'I've jotted down a few basics for now.' He handed it across the table to her.

While she read, he got on with his meal.

Lally finished the last of her tomato and egg while she read through the duties list. Though his gaze wasn't on her, she felt his consciousness of her, and had to force herself to concentrate on the words in front of her.

The list included taking care of his laundry, cleaning the apartment, meals and changing the linens. She would be in charge of his mobile phone during the hours he was writing, take messages and make the decision as to whether to interrupt him or not depending on what messages came through from his Sydney business.

There were a few lines about how to deal with the work crew, but he mostly wanted to handle that for himself.

'That all seems very reasonable.' Lally glanced up.

'I may ask for other duties as time progresses. Once the crew begins to get the apartments up to speed, I may send you in to clean them ready for occupation.'

'I'll be glad to do that.' Lally wanted to work hard for him. 'I like to keep busy. The task doesn't matter, just so long as I'm occupied.'

Had she made herself sound boring?

Why would it matter if you had, Latitia? You're his housekeeper. You don't have to be interesting, just productive and helpful.

'I'm good at multi-tasking through phone calls.' Lally's phone usually ran hot with calls and text messages. Yet, in the beaded bag at her feet, her phone was still and silent. The contact from her family had all but stopped since Lally had realised she was going to have to go outside normal channels to look for a job.

A man in a hard hat strode across the courtyard towards them. He stopped just short of their table. 'Morning, Mr Travers. Sorry to interrupt, but I'm ready to discuss these plans any time you are.' He gestured to the clipboard in his other hand. 'The crew should be in this morning to start the work to get that swimming pool up to speed too. They'll have to drain it, to do the work to turn it into a heated pool, but the water's too far gone to fix by shocking it with chlorine and balancing agents, so you're not losing anything on that score.'

Cam glanced towards the building. 'What other plans are on for today?'

'Makes the most sense to strip all the apartments at once, so that's what we'll be doing.' The man's gaze shifted to Lally and lingered. 'We, eh, you don't need any of the other apartments until all the work is done, so this'll streamline the process.'

'Thank you.' The words emerged in a deeper than usual cadence. Cam frowned and then said, 'Let me introduce you. Jordan Hayes, this is my housekeeper, Lally Douglas. Lally, meet my site manager.'

The man stuck out a hand. 'Nice to meet you.'

Lally shook his hand, reclaimed her own, and got to her feet. 'I'll leave you both to your discussion. I'd like to get started on my workload.' Her gaze shifted to the breakfast table. 'I'll clear this away once I've settled my belongings inside.'

Lally slipped away before Cam could think of

anything to say in response, and then the site manager spoke and Cam forced his thoughts onto the work here.

Cam didn't want to examine the tight feeling that had invaded his chest when Lally had slipped her hand into the other man's grip. If that reaction had been possessive, Cam had no right to it. His mouth tightened. He did his best to relax his expression as he spoke to the manager. 'We'll go into my office and talk there. It will be a bit quieter.'

Perhaps if he tucked himself away in there after this talk—focused on the property development, checked in with his Sydney office for the morning and then attacked his writing—he would get his thoughts off fixating on a certain brand-new, temporarily employed housekeeper.

For the truth was she had looked far too good when she'd arrived this morning, pulling a bunch of suitcases along behind her while her hips swayed and her legs ate up the ground beneath her feet in long strides. Cam had noticed how good she looked, far too much.

It was one thing to do such minor and insignificant things as notice the shape of her hands, he told himself, but that noticing had to stop.

Cam led the way into his office, the site manager behind him.

He would put Lally Douglas right out of his mind and not think about her again until lunch-time.

It wasn't as though he couldn't control his mild attraction to her. How ridiculous would that be?

CHAPTER THREE

'YOU'RE quite sure you're okay, Aunt Edie?' Lally had her mobile phone jammed between her shoulder and her ear. It felt right there, and so it should. Usually she spent a lot of her day with a phone in that exact position, talking with one relative or another while she went about her work and various family members checked in with her.

Today she'd had to phone Auntie herself; she had only received a couple of text messages all morning, mostly from two of her teenage cousins who'd recently got their first-ever mobile phones.

Of course, she'd been kept busy with calls and a few text messages coming in to Cam's mobile. It felt a little intimate to take all his calls and messages. What if a woman phoned?

And what if the phone he gave her was purely

for business and he had another one for his social life? Lots of people did that.

Right. Why was Lally fixating on Cam's social life, anyway? She should be fixating on her family's silence. Lally had kept so close to all her family in the past. It felt unsettling now not to hear from them much.

'You're working an outside job,' she muttered. 'They probably don't want to call and disturb that.'

'Beg pardon, dear?'

'Oh, sorry, Auntie. It was nothing; I was just talking to myself.' She was talking to Auntie, who seemed quite happy to talk, so what was Lally worrying about anyway?

Lally whisked eggs in a bowl and quickly poured the results over a selection of cooked vegetables in a heated pan on the stove. 'Promise me you're well, Auntie. You're taking all your meds? You've got Nova coming over to sort them out for you for the start of each day? Because I could drive over at night during my time off.'

'I'm fine, Lally. Nova comes every day, but even if she didn't I could cope. You just enjoy your work out there in the world where you might meet—' Her aunt coughed. 'We all think you'll do a very good job, just as you always do, dear.'

'Thank you. I appreciate that.' And Lally did. She was being quite silly to feel displaced. For heaven's sake, she'd only been at the new job for half a day. By the end of the week she might be getting so many calls and messages from her family that her new boss would be quite angry with her, if he didn't see that she always kept working throughout those calls and messages, hard and at speed.

And, of course, she would put answering his mobile first.

Lally had learned a long time ago to multi-task. Cameron seemed to live that way too. It was something they had in common.

What you have in common is that he's the boss and you're the employee, Lally. Try to remember that!

'Shouldn't you be focusing on your new job this morning, Lally?' Auntie asked the words into the silence, almost as though she'd read Lally's mind.

'I am.' Lally glanced around the kitchen. Cam

had left no mess, so it had been easy to give the whole area a deep clean. Now Lally sprinkled fresh, chopped herbs into the frittata and turned it down to heat through.

With a light salad, that would take care of their lunch, and this afternoon she'd see about their dinner. So far she'd cleaned most of the rooms, settled her things into the room across the small hall from Cameron's bedroom, looked over the pantry supplies, made a list of things she would need to buy soon and organised this meal.

And had taken Cameron's messages. None of them had sounded unbearably urgent, though the content of many of them from his Sydney office had brought it home to Lally that Cameron truly dealt in big dollars.

Lally prepared the salad with cherry tomatoes, lettuce, mushroom slices and slivers of avocado mixed with a tangy dressing; that job was done. She checked on the frittata; it was almost cooked.

Sam had liked tangy dressing on his salad.

The thought slid sideways into Lally's mind; it wasn't welcome. She so rarely thought about

Sam. If getting out and working with a man would make that a common occurrence, Lally was not going to be pleased. 'I'm working and talking at once, Auntie. I can talk. Tell everyone else they can call me too. Even if just early in the mornings, or in the evenings, if they're worried that much about my job. I'm sure I can fit in some calls—'

But her aunt had already rushed out a, 'Love you,' and disconnected the call at her end.

Well!

Lally drew a deep breath. 'It might have been nice to get to say "I love you" back—'

'Whatever that is, it smells wonderful.' The deep words sounded over the top of hers and cut them off abruptly. 'Sorry, were you on the phone?'

'Oh. I didn't realise you were there.' She'd been talking out loud like a loon. 'Um, no, I'm all finished with my phone call. It was my phone that time, but I have a heap of messages from yours.'

'On the phone to the boyfriend?' Cam's words were unruffled, and yet something in his tone made Lally seek his gaze.

His eyes were shielded by those long, silky lashes.

'I should have brought this up at our interview. I apologise that I didn't, but I'll cover it now.' She did feel guilty, even though there was no need. 'I like to speak with family members when I have a moment. I'll do it discreetly, I won't disrupt you in any way, and I always keep working. I can assure you I don't lose any work time or concentration over the calls I make, and of course I'll always use my own phone.'

'Family.' Cameron's expression was complex. He ran his fingers through his short hair. 'Of course that's not a problem. You're welcome to keep whatever contact you need.'

'Thank you.' Lally considered telling him there was no boyfriend, but he'd probably figured that out anyway. In any case, it wasn't important. 'I appreciate you being understanding about my need for contact with my family.'

Now, if Lally could just get her *family* to come back on board with that contact.

'I can see you've been busy.' Cameron's glance roved the kitchen, dining room and lounge areas, before it came back to rest on her, and his expression softened. 'Thank you for what you've done already to help make me comfortable.'

'That's what I'm here for.' But his praise and appreciation wrapped around her just the same.

Being needed: it was an issue for Lally. She knew it; she would even admit it. Until now she'd thought it was all just about family relationships for her.

And it was. This just felt sort of similar because she was helping him, too, and that was what she did for them. Her happiness certainly had nothing to do with that softening of his expression when his gaze rested on her. She wasn't looking for tenderness from him, for goodness' sake; that would be ridiculous.

Lally was too wary to consider something like that with a man again anyway. And she was still young, she justified to herself. She had plenty of time to think about getting back into the dating game. And she'd been really busy with family commitments.

Busy enough that they might have pushed her out so she'd find time for a social life again?

Her family had been known to stick their noses into each other's lives at times. Lally had been guilty of it too. In a big, loving family that would always happen, and she'd had her share of them hinting that she could do with getting out more.

But they wouldn't take it this far, would they? Of course they wouldn't…

'Lunch is almost ready now, if you want to take a seat in the dining room.' Lally would far rather eat lunch than go on thinking about that topic. She gestured to the freshly polished dining-table. 'Or we can eat outside, if you'd prefer? It's frittata. I hope that's okay.'

'Inside will be fine, and I eat most things.' He paused and the hint of a smile lifted the edges of his mouth. 'No artichoke. Other than that, I'm very agreeable about food.'

'That will make cooking for you a dream. I'd like to take advantage of the fresh markets for produce for a lot of our meals.' She wanted to feed him on the freshest items available, because she thought it might help with whatever had been exhausting him—lack of sleep, long hours, book stress, whatever the problem. Even if it didn't, it would put his body in a good place, health-wise.

Yes, fine, she was acting like a little mother. Why not, when she'd had a hundred or so relatives to practice those skills on? They all deserved to be loved to bits and looked after as much as possible, especially considering how much they'd had to put up with from her.

Not that she felt the need to earn their love. Well, that would be just silly, wouldn't it? And she didn't feel like a little mother; she felt like a determined housekeeper.

Lally turned the frittata onto a serving plate, carried it and the salad to the table she'd set, and took her seat. 'I hope you'll eat while the food is hot and at its best, and have as much as you want. I made plenty. I do have a bunch of messages from your phone, but I think they can all wait until after you've eaten.'

Now she sounded as though she was very generously allowing him to eat his own food, and making his work-related choices for him while she was at it. 'What if your editor rings?' Lally asked suddenly. 'Or your agent?'

'You'll be able to tell if they need to speak to me urgently, otherwise they can wait.' He gave a wry smile. 'I'm too professional to ask you to dodge them on my behalf if they phone and then ask for a progress update—though there might be certain days when I'll be tempted to do that if things keep going the way they have for the past few weeks.'

'You can't help it if you're in the middle of a sticky patch with your muse,' Lally declared. 'These things happen. It must be quite amazing to be internationally famous too. You probably have fans chasing after you and everything. Lots of women—'

The words burst out of her and Lally's face flooded with heat.

'I can't say I've been particularly *chased,* at least not to my knowledge.' Cam drawled the words. He felt far too pleased that Lally's words—when she'd got to the 'women' part of her statement—had sounded as though she was quite jealous at the thought of such a thing happening.

Two seconds later he realised that wasn't exactly the response he should have to her. And he didn't *want* women chasing him; he'd rather go and find them when he felt the need.

Cam helped himself to a piece of the frittata and some salad and took a first bite. The frittata was perfect, the accompanying salad the exact counterpoint for it; the zing of tangy dressing hit Cam's tongue, completing the experience. 'Did you make the dressing yourself? Where did you learn your cooking skills?'

'I did make the dressing. I learned to cook from two parents who both love it, and do it very differently but equally as well.' Lally's smile softened at whatever memories were in her head. 'What they didn't actively teach me, I guess I've learned by observation anyway.'

She seemed to take her skill level as nothing out of the ordinary.

'Your father runs a restaurant; I momentarily forgot that.' She'd told him that at their interview, and Cam had spent a few moments piecing together her family history in his mind. Torres-Strait Aboriginal mother, Italian father; the surname of 'Douglas' suggested that her father might not be fully Italian.

'Dad's mother married a Scotsman, just to keep things interesting.' Lally's lovely smile lit her face again.

'You have a diverse family tree.' Cam returned the smile, and gestured to his plate. 'The food is delicious, thank you. I think I've struck it lucky with you, Lally, if this meal and the work you've got through already are any indication.'

'You're welcome for all of it.' Her skin didn't show a blush. Yet somehow he suspected one had just happened—by the change to the sparkle in her eyes, perhaps?

What would she be like in the middle of passion?

Cam cut the thought off. The answer to that question was that it was not his business to wonder.

'I've done as much work as I could this morning.' Lally seemed flustered as she pulled the duties list from her pocket and flattened it on the table beside her plate. She glanced at it and raised her gaze to his face. 'I'll do all that I can to look after you, help you start to feel more rested and focus on what you need to do with your time.'

'I appreciate that.' Surely in another week or two he would get back to sleeping at least the four to four-and-a-half hours a night he usually got? Cam didn't expect Lally to be able to do a thing about that. Why would she? All the experts had failed to give him any long-term solutions that didn't involve knocking himself out at night with medications he didn't want to let become a habit in his life.

'I haven't forgotten about book research.' Her finger rested on a point on the list. 'I'm ready to help you with that in any way required.'

'I have a research project for you for after lunch, actually.' Cam went on to explain what he needed. 'I have two laptop computers. What I'd like you to do is use the second laptop and get the prohibition laws about using these substances in this state…' He jotted the names of several chemical compounds onto the bottom of her list.

'I'll do the rest of the research myself. Some of it has to be handled carefully; I don't want you dealing with anything that could be potentially dangerous to you.' He paused. 'At least I can still make forward progress with my lead character's investigations and activities to some degree, even if other aspects of the story are being difficult.'

Lally's eyes widened and her soft lips parted. '*You* take care with your research? You keep yourself safe?' Her words were so genuine, filled with concern for him.

Cam got that strange feeling in his chest again. 'Always. I always take care.' He was even more determined to take care of *her* in this admittedly small way.

As their gazes met and held, Cam was very conscious of her.

She was conscious of him. It was there in her guarded expression, the rejection and the self-protectiveness in every line of her body, and didn't fully manage to conceal the interest beneath.

They threw sparks off each other, and Lally didn't want to feel those sparks.

Were they for him? Or for any man at the moment?

And, either way, *why?*

But he didn't need to know why; Cam told himself this. He needed to develop a three-dimensional book character, not know every aspect of his new housekeeper's make-up.

They both dropped their gazes at the same time and Cam rubbed his face wearily.

'Are you okay, Cam? You mentioned you don't sleep well—I assumed that was due to stress or work pressures.' Lally's soft words impinged on his thoughts. 'If there's anything else I need to know…'

'I'm a long-term insomniac. It's annoying sometimes but it's nothing to worry about.'

Though he didn't care who knew about it one way or another, this wasn't something he discussed often. Cam wouldn't have held the answer back from her, though, not when her face had filled with such concern.

Lally gave a nod of acknowledgement. 'It's no wonder you felt like being spoiled a little. Maybe you can enjoy some more rest than usual, even if it doesn't come in the form of sleep.'

'Maybe I will. I've got my eye on the pool.' He shrugged his shoulders. 'A swim now and then would be relaxing.' He hesitated. 'If you hear me up and about in the middle of the night…'

'Do you like company at those times, or to be by yourself?' Lally's expression had softened so much, it was almost as though she needed to find a chink in his armour and felt somehow re-assured by finding it. 'I'd be happy to heat you some warm milk or sit up and talk.'

Cam pictured them sitting at this table at midnight. Somehow he doubted that drinking milk or talking would be the first things on his mind. He'd be thinking about kissing his way up the slender column of her neck until he reached those luscious lips and closed his own over them.

The urge to kiss her now, right in this blink of time, silenced him for a moment. It was one thing to imagine, even to want, but this urge felt somehow to be more than that.

Maybe you should just ask her if she'd curl up on the sofa with you, with your head in her lap, and stroke your face with her fingers until you fall asleep, you big baby.

Or you could admit you find her more than a little intriguing and that you're not doing a very good job of pushing back that interest.

All right, he did find her intriguing, but he

wasn't about to act on it. Theirs was a working relationship and that was exactly how Cam wanted it to be.

And that left how he wanted to deal with the rest of the day. And the next.

Cam cleared his throat and side-stepped the question. 'I'll take you to the market tomorrow morning and we can buy fresh produce together. I'll be awake anyway, so it makes sense that I go with you the first time at least.'

He could tell her what foods he liked the most, could carry her basket for her.

Or throw down his cloak for her to step on if she came across a puddle in her path!

'Excuse me.' He got to his feet and assured himself the only thought on his mind was getting back to business.

He was not running; he was planning and re-treating so he could focus on his book. A totally different thing.

Cam took Lally's written list of phone messages and the phone itself from the table. 'I'll see to these and drop the phone out to you before I start writing, if that's okay?'

'Thanks.' Lally glanced down at the notes he'd written for her to research. 'And I'll bring my research results to you as soon as I have them.'

Cam looked at the sweep of her long black lashes. 'Other than that, perhaps you can just keep going with your housekeeping jobs.' If Cam stayed clear for a few hours, maybe he would get these strange reactions to her sorted out a little better.

Lally rose and started to gather dishes into capable hands. 'Good luck with the writing.'

'Thanks.'

Cam nodded and left.

CHAPTER FOUR

'I MEANT to unpack all this as soon as we got home.' It was the next afternoon. Lally reached into one of the string bags sitting on the kitchen counter in the apartment and pulled out several canned goods.

Her voice was raised a little to be heard over the outside noise of the refurbishing crew. Cam had to admit that right now they sounded more like a destruction mob. 'Are you okay with that noise? It's not driving you crazy?'

'Oh, no,' she said. 'I'm fine with it. If anything would get to me, I think it would be too much quiet.'

Cam understood that only too well. Maybe noise was what he needed at night.

You've tried that, remember? You've tried every trick there is. Noise or no noise; light or dark; quiet or loud; whatever, you don't sleep beyond what your body has to have to survive. That's all there is to it.

He returned his gaze to his housekeeper. 'You got busy when we got back here.' Lally had called it 'home' and hadn't seemed to notice the word. But in truth where did Lally Douglas call 'home'? She'd told him she had a room at her parents' home; was that it? At twenty-four, didn't she want her freedom at some point?

And why did it even matter to Cam? 'Home,' he'd never had. A faceless, nameless apartment in the centre of Sydney that he visited now and then hardly counted.

Yet wouldn't it be nice to have a home? A real one? With a permanent housekeeper like Lally to look after him?

Dumb thought, Travers. This was a temporary measure, nothing more. Cam drew a breath. 'There's nothing in the foodstuffs that will have spoiled.'

'No. I put the perishables away straight off, at least.' Lally removed the remaining articles from the bags and started to pack them into the larder.

Cam resisted the urge to help. He'd crossed the line enough by insisting they shop together at the market first thing this morning. When they'd got back, he'd eaten breakfast with her—then had taken himself off to his office and proceeded to give his hero's love-interest so many of Lally Douglas's traits and characteristics that he'd had to delete half the work he'd written.

So he'd deleted, and he'd wrestled with his story some more, and he'd come up with what he knew was a great scene-idea—but then he couldn't get that to work either. Without realising he did it, Cam heaved a sigh.

'Is the writing not going well?' Lally's words were empathetic.

He shook his head. 'I've got a scene planned in my mind, but when I try to write it I can't visualise it properly. I can't "see" the heroine in my mind's eye. I'm not sure how to use their surroundings. It's a scene that I know will work, but I can't seem to *get* it to work. I think as long as the heroine remains shadowy in my mind, this problem is going to continue.'

'What would bring her to life for you?' Lally's

eyebrows drew together as she considered the matter. 'Could you "interview" her? Ask her questions to get to know her?'

'Stream-of-consciousness interviewing? I did try that about a week ago, but I didn't get anywhere with it.' Cam forced himself not to scowl his irritation over this. 'I feel as though I need to somehow throw her into the middle of this scene, really get in deep there with her. Once I see how she reacts, the pieces will all come together. Maybe.'

'Hmm.' Lally was silent for a long moment. She tipped her head to the side and tapped her finger on her chin before her eyes lit up. 'When Mum gets stuck on a painting, she tells my aunt the concept. Auntie takes a sheet of paper and whips out her interpretation of how she'd do the painting. Mum invariably says that's *not* how the idea should be executed! Rejecting one idea helps Mum to figure out how *she* wants to execute it.'

'That's an interesting concept.' It was Cam's turn to frown. 'I'd try that, if there was a chance it would rattle loose *my* interpretation. But how?'

'You need a "volunteer from the audience".' The smile deepened on Lally's lovely mouth. 'Someone, or more than one person, to act out the scene for you. You don't have to like how they do it, but it might help you figure out what you *do* want for the scene.'

Cam gave a surprised laugh. 'That could just work. I'd have to find an acting society or a theatre group willing to act it.'

'Or you and I could do it.' The words came out in a little rush and she immediately bit her lip. 'Not if you didn't want us to, but if you didn't want the hassle of trying to find real actors—if you only needed to play-act it to help you figure it out—we could do that, couldn't we?'

'We could.' Her enthusiasm started to spread through him too. 'My idea is a wheels-within-wheels kind of situation, where he's pretending interest in her but he suspects her of being a double agent or spy or assassin. He thinks if he disarms her with food, wine and attention he'll figure out what she's up to.' He went on. 'She's got an equal number of suspicions about him. She pretends to be "buyable" for the night, to gain access to his hotel room to search it later, and then she's going to disappear—but he lures her to the roof top of the building after dinner when he suspects her motives are as duplicitous as his are.'

Cam drew a breath. 'Before dinner he spends money on her, buying her a dress and other gifts.'

'It really is wheels within wheels.' Lally's eyes were like stars. 'Oh, but that sounds so exciting. We could role-play the whole evening from beginning to end. It wouldn't have to be an exact match, but it could be a lot of fun!'

'Let's do it.' Cam's smile spread until it was as wide as hers. 'It'll have to be late in the day. If we're going to do this I want the right atmosphere, time of night, all of it.'

Happiness filled her face. 'Tonight?'

Cam couldn't seem to look away from that happiness. 'Yes, we'll do it tonight. We'll leave here at seven p.m. I'd better get on the computer and figure out where we can go that will provide the kind of backdrop I want.' He started to turn away; he *had* to turn away. 'Can you manage that?'

'Of course.' She did a little bounce on the balls

of her feet. 'I'll go on with other work until you're ready for us to leave.'

He looked at her and tried not to think about the curve of the side of her face, her cheek, her chin and her lush lips that looked soft and kissable. 'We'll be out until around midnight, so feel free to take some time off this afternoon before we leave. I don't want to over-tire you.'

'I'll take a nap for an hour if I can get to sleep,' Lally conceded, but with a glow of anticipation still all over her face.

Somehow Cam doubted she would relax into sleep in this mood, but he wasn't a good one to gauge her chances. Just because he wouldn't have been able to sleep in the afternoon didn't mean she might not be able to nod off any time she decided she wanted to.

'I'll see you at seven.' He glanced at her clothes. 'You can come dressed as you are now, or in something similar; it doesn't really matter. Choosing clothes in the same way the female character would do that tonight will be part of our role-play. I'll need to locate a big hotel that has boutique stores. We'll shop there, enact the time in the dining room, and then go up on the rooftop for that part.'

Her eyes widened. 'It—it won't cost you a lot, will it? I didn't mean to suggest…'

'Something that might get my writing back on track after weeks of it driving me crazy because I haven't been able to get there?' He felt lighter than he had in all those weeks. 'If it costs me a little to organise this evening and I get a result, I will be more than happy, so don't give that another thought. Whatever I spend I'll be able to tax-deduct, anyway.'

'Well, I guess.' Lally frowned. 'Make sure it's a hotel that does clothing hire, or has cheap stores. We can go through the motions, buy or hire what we have to, I guess, but keep the expense right down.'

Cam smiled at the earnest face looking at him. 'You need to think of it as a cross between Cinderella and—I don't know—winning a shopping spree or something.'

'Oh, well, okay. I guess.'

'Good.' Cam turned away. 'I'll see you when it's time to go.'

* * *

'This is it. The boutique shops inside should provide what we need.' Cam spoke to Lally as he handed his car keys to a parking valet. He paused on the footpath that led into the hotel itself.

Lally drew a big breath. 'So we're all set for our night's acting. Oh, I hope it'll be fun, and you'll go back later and your story will just pour out of your fingertips because your imagination will have worked out what you want to do. The hotel looks awfully fancy.'

Her anticipation was so sweet that Cam just had to smile. Lally might enjoy wearing some different clothes, too, he thought with a hint of fondness that crept up on him. She dressed nicely already, but sometimes he felt she dressed to try not to be noticed. 'I haven't fully explained the final part of the evening when we'll go up on the rooftop: you'll be entirely safe, but I need an unanticipated reaction out of you. If you don't mind.'

'Your mysteriousness is making my imagination run wild.' Lally admitted this with a smile as she met Cam's gaze. 'I don't mind. You can surprise me. That can be part of the fun too.'

Cam cleared his throat. 'Thanks for being a

good sport about it. You truly won't mind being dressed up and having your hair and make-up done?'

'Hair and make-up too?' Her eyes widened. 'I imagine I'll feel as though I'm being thoroughly spoiled.'

Lally gave her answer to Cameron and tried to gather her concentration. Cinderella; he'd said to think of it as that.

Her boss in a dinner suit; that was a big part of the reason for her distraction. In truth, Lally did feel like Cinderella—well, Cinderella with a slightly weary but anticipation-filled prince at her side.

A prince who looked divine clothed this way, and wore his exhaustion more attractively than should be legal.

When she'd first emerged from her room and seen Cameron waiting for her, Lally's pulse had raced.

'Thank you for agreeing to this,' he'd said, and clasped her hand briefly before leading the way outside to his car. Beautiful car, gorgeous driver. Cameron had relaxed her with easy conversation during the trip, and even now as they walked through the hotel he somehow made her feel special whether he was looking all about him to research his book or not.

A night out of time, that was what this would be for Lally. She could do it, of course she could, and have a whole lot of fun in the process!

Cam led her straight to the grouping of boutique clothing-stores with fashionably sparse window-displays. Lally glanced around the opulent hotel's interior; that opulence tied in with what she saw here. A qualm struck; she leaned towards Cam and whispered urgently, 'That looks like a *designer original* dress in the window.'

'It is, but from my research there are plenty of non-designer dresses in the shop as well.' Cam stepped inside without giving Lally a chance to argue it one way or another. 'And here's our shop assistant ready to help us.'

'But the money,' Lally whispered, and tugged on his arm. 'It *all* looks expensive. You can't…'

He turned and gave a reassuring smile. 'These purchases are a legitimate business expense. I'll claim them against tax, and I get to give a great housekeeper the gift of a few things after we've used them for my research—if you'd like them. You'll let me do that rather than throwing them out, won't you?'

'Throw?' Lally bit back a gasp. He wanted her to let him buy the things and then give them to her, but she'd thought if that happened it would be in a very inexpensive way.

'It's not hurting anything, Lally.' He said it in such a businesslike way. 'I need this kind of setting. You understand?'

Lally calmed down a little. This was just work, when all was said and done. Unusual, maybe, but still work.

If her awareness of him suggested differently, well, she would get that sorted out. She would. She'd just watch very carefully to make sure they didn't end up buying a dress that cost a ridiculous amount of money.

'Good evening. How may I help you?' The saleswoman was already sizing Lally up.

'We need a dress. Something bright, flattering and elegant; a handbag; earrings, and I think…' Cam's gaze shifted to Lally's neck and lingered there. 'Yes, a necklace. I'll know what I want for that once we choose the dress. Hmm…' He turned to the saleswoman.

'I don't know much about this, but something that will suit her colouring, bring out the brown of her eyes and make the most of her hair. That's what I want.'

You should be in colours, Latitia. You were born for them on all sides of your family tree!

Mum had said that to her—recently, actually, now Lally thought of it. She had given Lally an almost disappointed look when Lally had shrugged her shoulders and said she preferred plain colours, and shades that blended rather than stood out. Mum had looked away and muttered something about 'long-term hibernation behaviour.'

A week later Lally had finished working at the fishing-tackle-and-bait store, and she'd no longer been needed in the next job she'd had lined up in the family. The whole family had been just fine getting along without her, and she'd ended up with Cam.

Now they were shopping, and he had his

arm loosely against her shoulders; when had that happened?

Lally looked away in case she was gaping over the list he'd just given the saleswoman. Lally's glance fell on a mirror on the shop-wall that showed their reflections. Cam had a spark of enjoyment in his eyes.

Worse was the corresponding sparkle in her eyes.

More dangerous still was how much she liked the look of those two reflections; side by side.

Lally could count on one hand the number of times she'd been out on a date since the disaster of Sam six years ago. The last time must have been over a year ago. Those dates had been pleasant enough, she supposed, but in a very controlled way for her, and she'd never looked for a repeat.

Her reaction just now hadn't felt controlled. Plus, this was *not* a date!

'Nothing designer,' Lally said with about as much spine in her tone as an overcooked noodle. She cleared her throat and tried again. 'Maybe you have a sale rack?'

'Perish *that* thought.' The sales lady said it

with good humour, disappeared for a moment and returned with a garment over her arm. 'Perhaps you'd like to try this? It's middle range, though it's an odd thing to be told *not* to include designer choices!' She held up a flow of deep-red silk.

'Oh, it's…gorgeous.' The words poured out of Lally's mouth before she could stop them; to her credit she tried to back-pedal as soon as it happened. 'That is, I'm not sure. It's awfully noticeable—the colour and style…' Lally broke off and turned to Cam. 'I guess that doesn't matter. It's only to help you to figure out what you want.'

'That's right. It seems…as good a choice as any.' He nodded. 'I'm having fun, Lally, and that's got to be good for my muse. So, go and try the dress on, please.'

'It will make you look absolutely radiant, dear.' Somehow the woman had her hustled through the store and into a changing room with the dress pushed into her hands before Lally quite realised what had happened. Her last glimpse before the dressing room door closed was of Cam turning to examine a shelf of evening bags with a purposeful and cheerful glint in his eyes.

Lally locked the dressing-room door, turned to the mirror, and saw a bright-eyed girl with red silk clutched in her hands.

'It won't fit,' she muttered, not sure if she was being hopeful, practical, hedging her bets or trying to talk herself out of a love affair that had already taken wings the moment the saleswoman held up the dress.

'You're such a predictable female, Lally.' She muttered the words beneath her breath. 'The first time someone throws a pretty dress at you, and all your past decisions about fashion choices and colours go out the window.'

Oh, but this was different. This wasn't for *her,* not really. This was for research so Cam could look at Lally and choose a whole different look for his book character.

It was reverse psychology, and it would work; Lally just knew it would. Lally was just the human mannequin for the evening, as cardboard and one-dimensional as could be.

She was filled with a lot of excitement for someone who was one dimensional, though.

'Are you done?' Cam's voice sounded from outside the cubicle. 'May I see the dress on you?'

Lally was done. She'd simply been standing there staring mutely at the transformation that had appeared in the mirror. She didn't feel much like a mannequin; she felt like a girl in a gorgeous dress.

'I'm not sure if this…' Lally put her hand on the door latch, unlocked it and pulled it open.

'You…' The single word trailed away as Cam's gaze slowly travelled from her head to her toes and back again.

'It seems to be the right size.' Lally resisted the urge to fidget with the hem or twitch the fabric over her hips. The dress fitted like a glove and flowed over her curves in all the right ways.

'It's perf— That is, I'm sure it'll be fine for our purpose, to help me figure out what the heroine in the story would wear.' Cam gave one slow blink and his voice deepened as he held out his hand. 'Put these on with it, please.'

A drop-necklace and set of dangling earrings were settled into the palm of her hand, and her fingers were curled closed over them. 'I slipped out to the jewellery store beside this one while you changed into the dress.'

'Okay, well, I'll put them on.' Their fingers brushed as Lally made sure she had a proper grip on the items.

Her heart was pounding. It was so stupid, but she fell silent as she withdrew her hand. Had Cam's hand moved away quite slowly, as though he might have been almost reluctant to lose the contact?

'There's a bag too.' His voice was deep and he cleared his throat before he went on. 'I'll give that to you when you come out.'

Lally could have put the necklace and earrings on in front of him, but she was rather glad for a moment to herself. She had to pull herself together.

The earrings were simple gold with a pearl drop that bumped against her neck when she moved her head. The matching pearl-drop necklace nestled between her breasts. It would have been difficult to find a set to create a better foil for the dress.

No, Lally, it suits you and *the dress perfectly.*

Lally tucked her hair behind her ears to

showcase the earrings. They really needed an upswept hairstyle; so did the dress. Lally took another proper look in the mirror.

The dress was deep red with a crossover V-neckline that cupped her breasts. It was deceptively simple, clinging in beautifully cut lines until it fell in loose folds to just below her knees. The hem was handkerchief-cut and swirled as she moved.

Cameron had dressed her the way she would have dressed herself six years ago. No; he'd dressed her the way that eighteen-year-old would have dressed six years on if she hadn't hidden herself in bland colours.

She hadn't *hidden* herself. She'd outgrown colours.

Have you, Lally? Because you look great in this, vibrant and alive and ready to take on the world. Ready to participate *in the world, not avoid it from within the heart of your family.*

Oh, this was silly! Lally was helping Cam; they were doing research. She wanted to get on with that and leave these other thoughts behind her. He'd look at all this, and it might look good on her, but it would help him see how he wanted to dress his heroine. He might put his character in faux fur, or shiny pink plastic, or dress her in blue velvet.

Lally gathered her other clothes into her hands, flung the door open and stepped out. She joined Cam at the service counter where he'd just finished paying for his transaction. 'I'm ready to get on with the rest of our research.'

And *that* was what this was truly all about.

CHAPTER FIVE

'THE hairdresser is next.' Cam made this announcement and led Lally towards the hotel salon. He pressed a small sparkly bag into her hands as they walked. His other hand held a bag the saleswoman had kindly supplied for Lally's day clothes. 'In the scene, the female character would make out that she wanted to be showered with as much "spoiling" as she could get.'

'And your male lead would be determined to do that, to keep her suspicions at bay about his real motives. They'll be deep in their false roles.' Lally took the small bag; she couldn't take her eyes from his face. The grooves at the sides of his mouth were deep. His face had the kind of stillness that concealed attraction and awareness.

Though she knew she shouldn't, though there were a thousand reasons why it would be better if she failed to react to this at all, Lally's gaze locked with his. Her fingers closed about the short strap of the bag, she drew a deep, deep breath and admitted, to herself at least, that she was equally attracted to Cam. That had to stop right now. They had to get the fun back and avoid these other inappropriate responses to each other. It was probably just the atmosphere getting to both of them, anyway.

Somehow Lally got through the appointment with the hair stylist. It helped that Cam sat on a lounge in the waiting area and buried his nose in a magazine.

Half an hour later Lally got up from the chair with her curls artfully drawn away from her face in a high pony-tail with just a few tendrils trailing down her back.

'Shoes.' Cameron murmured the single word as his gaze tracked over her hair and the vulnerable nape of her neck.

'You'll have to decide about your heroine's hair,' Lally said, and hoped the desperate edge couldn't be heard in her tone. 'It's probably ice-blonde, straight and swept up in a bun away from her model-gorgeous face.'

'Uh, yes. Perhaps.' Cam drew her to a shoe shop.

Lally's transformation to Cinderella-dressed-for-the-ball reached its final moment as they stepped through the door. She spotted the sandals immediately. They were third row down on an elegant stand, they had their own name—Grace After Midnight—and she had to have them.

Six inch stiletto gold-and-black heels; tiny criss-cross gold-and-black strips across the instep. Elegant ankle straps. All of Lally's sensible thoughts and cautions disintegrated for that moment of time. She forgot the purpose of the night, forgot everything—well, not Cam, but he did take second place to the shoes for a minute.

'I'll pay for these myself.' They were in her hands before she finished speaking the words, on her feet moments later. They fit like a dream; these shoes were meant to be.

Lally had her credit card and there were fifty dollars in the pocket of the skirt that had gone into the dress shop bag with her other clothes. She held her hand out to Cam. He came back into focus, and so did his grin that held outright amusement—was that a hint of enchantment?

Of course it isn't, Lally. It so totally isn't! 'I need the bag, please.'

'No. I've got this.' Cam paid for the shoes and hustled her out of the store.

'You don't understand. I had to have them, you see.' How did she explain the compulsion that took a pair of shoes from stage prop to girl's best friend? And how that meant she couldn't let him pay for her pure indulgence.

'And I'd have paid that much or more for any choice that you made.' With those few words, Cam dismissed the matter.

And he truly did dismiss it. The glint in his eyes was a good-humoured one, but it also warned her that arguing would be futile. He tucked her arm through his and led her towards the hotel's restaurant. 'You look great, Lally. You're made for bright colours.'

'That's what Mum says.' *Business, Lally!* She must remember tonight was about his work, no matter how he'd been looking at her or how it felt to walk at his side and feel as though she were made to belong there.

'Over dinner we'll discuss where this has put

you in terms of figuring out your heroine,' Lally declared, and led the way with determination towards their dining table.

Lally looked amazing; the thought washed through Cam yet again as he escorted his house-keeper into the restaurant. She looked amazing, was dressed amazingly and walked incredibly in heels that would have stopped a lot of women in their tracks.

He'd told Lally she was made for colours. What he hadn't said was that she was made for all of this—the dress, the shoes, the lovely hair, the sparkle in her eyes…

Yes, he had needed this research for his story. Seeing Lally in the clothes had somehow made her more vibrant and real to him, and that had, indeed, already helped him to start seeing his book's heroine.

Not an ice-blonde, but a woman in her late thirties with elegant looks and straight brunette hair in a cap-cut to her head. A woman who wore classic black. Lally's reverse-psychology theory was working. Her quirky approach to the problem had got him well on the way to re-solving it.

He'd thought that to fix his writer's block he needed a housekeeper to free up his time so he could concentrate better.

What he'd needed was tonight's insights.

'This way, please.' The waiter seated them with a flourish at the table Cam had booked earlier. The man's gaze rested for a long moment on Lally's beauty.

Cam could only silently agree.

'I feel quite transformed.' Lally's fingers toyed with the clasp of the small bag in her lap after the waiter walked away. 'Cinderella ready for the ball, except the shoes aren't glass.' Her lips pressed together. 'Well, this isn't about me. What would your book character be wearing? What would she have bought in the shop?'

'The shoes are better than glass.' They revealed the beauty of Lally's calf muscles, the delicate shape of her feet, the slender ankles. But that wasn't something Cam should tell his housekeeper. 'My heroine would be in a black dress. Full length and fitted. She's in black stiletto-shoes with a closed toe and heel—what do you call those?'

'Pumps?'

'Yes.' Cam nodded. 'She's wearing diamonds, a choker around her throat, a thick tennis-bracelet style of cuff on her right wrist. Earrings that are a carat apiece.'

'You're working her out! That's great.' Lally glanced down at the bag in her lap. 'The diamanté on this is amazing. It looks so real.'

Cam thought about avoiding her gaze when she raised it, but in the end he simply returned it and hoped he didn't look too guilty. Or too sheepish. 'They are real, but there aren't many, and they're very small. The bags with fake stones cost nearly as much.'

He added somewhat craftily, 'It's the perfect size for a small ladies' handgun.'

'Ooh.' Lally's eyes lit up and she leaned forward in her chair, her whole face alight with interest and excitement. 'Is she an assassin? A double agent?'

'Close to that.' He knew he was being mysteri-ous, but the desire to tease her just a little had got hold of him. Cam's gaze tracked over her hair and the sweep of her neck, the soft nape, and he forgot about his characters.

Instead, Cam wanted to kiss Lally right there at the base of her neck, to inhale the scent of her skin and brush his lips over the side of her neck and across her face. He felt ridiculously proud that he'd been able to distract her about the cost of the bag. 'Don't tell anyone what ideas I have in mind for the heroine.' He winked. 'I have to keep the book's secrets until it hits the shelves, otherwise my career as a writer is over.'

'I won't tell a soul.' She crossed her heart with her fingers, joining in the fun. 'I guess it's all right to confess I'm enjoying the dress, and I love the shoes. I had a pair that were similar when I was fresh out of high school.' Lally made this admission almost guiltily. 'They were cheaper, and not quite as pretty, but they made me feel…'

'Beautiful? You are.'

Maybe he shouldn't have said it—*probably* he shouldn't have said it—but the words were out.

'Thank you.' Lally registered Cam's words and tried not to let her feelings melt. If she simply felt complimented, that would be okay, still manageable. The charming man tells the girl she looks great, the girl appreciates his words of admiration and takes them for what they are: a compliment. The same as he might give to any other woman while they were working on an unusual project together.

But she didn't feel only complimented; she felt Cam's awareness of her, and hers of him. She felt the consciousness that flowed back and forth between them that had been beneath the surface from the start of the night, but hidden under the excitement and fun factor of their research and role-playing.

That consciousness *was* there. Even now as they sat here, Cam's upper body leaned forward as though he'd like to close the distance of the table that separated them and press a soft kiss to her lips.

Lally's body leaned in too, until she forcibly stopped herself and straightened her spine.

She had to remember that Cameron Travers

was her employer, not a man she would like to melt into, to kiss and be kissed by.

'We should choose something to eat.' Lally dropped her gaze to the menu; she flipped it open and stared blindly at the *entrées*. 'Do you need us to choose anything specific for research purposes?'

'No. Just choose what you'd like to eat.' Cam, too, turned his attention to his menu.

You see? They were being perfectly sensible.

Eventually the list of dishes unscrambled itself enough that Lally could read it: tuscan prawns; artichoke and sweet-potato soup—Cam would avoid that one—lamb, leek and bread broth; baked cheese bites in puff pastry with a dark-plum dipping sauce.

'I think I'll have the broth.' Lally rejected the appeal of spicy prawns, of sensually melted cheese in pastry. 'Yes, the broth. Something healthy and ordinary. It seems exactly what I'd like.'

She was a sensible, ordinary girl, after all, even if she had allowed herself to be swept up in the purchase of a lovely dress and a pair of stunning shoes.

Over all, Lally had progressed past being influenced by emotions, sudden whims or anything else uncontrolled.

Sam had taught her that lesson—well, in truth, the pain she had caused out of knowing him had taught her. Lally's good cheer wobbled.

In that moment Cam glanced at her, smiled and said softly, 'Thank you, Lally, for being such a good sport tonight. I've really enjoyed myself, enjoyed the research. I've got ideas coming into focus in my mind. You've helped me to get the muse back on track.'

'You're welcome. It's been my pleasure to help you.' Lally pushed those other unhappy thoughts far away.

Cameron's eyes moved over his menu, but a smile lingered on his face. After that he led the conversation onto the topic of his property development; maybe he knew she needed that easing of tension.

He talked about the challenge of obtaining good workers in locations all around Australia wherever he purchased properties to develop, and the properties themselves. Lally relaxed and her happiness came back.

'You've certainly developed some interesting projects over the years. Several of my family members might be interested in the art gallery you mentioned in the tourist township on the Queensland coast.' Some of them might like to have work exhibited there, if the gallery manager was interested.

Their *entrées* arrived and Lally dipped her spoon into the broth. It was thick with chunks of lamb, loaded with fresh colourful vegetables, and the aroma was spicy. She took the first taste onto her tongue and closed her eyes while the flavours exploded on her palate.

Cameron cut a piece from a Tuscan prawn, popped it into his mouth and chewed. He gestured towards her soup bowl. 'How is it?'

'Fabulously interesting and totally yummy.' Lally smiled in wry acceptance. She was wearing a beautiful red dress and killer heels—would it really hurt for her to eat exciting food too?

They talked about nothing much. It should have been totally unthreatening; instead, a rising consciousness seemed to fill the air between them once again until every breath she took held the essence of that consciousness, whether Lally felt ready to feel like that or not.

When Cam picked up his fork and knife, Lally realised they'd both been sitting there staring at each other in unmoving silence.

At what point had they put down their implements and simply sat in quiet stillness?

Almost…like lovers.

The way you used to stare at Sam across a dinner table, totally besotted, and with no thought for anything beyond the smooth words, smoother smiles and the looks he used to send your way?

'How, um, how would your heroine behave at this point of the evening?' They'd finished the *entrées;* Lally sipped her water and told herself she had to do better than this.

'Here we are.' A waiter deftly reordered their table setting and offered Cam a choice of wines to go with their main course. Cam had chosen flame-grilled steak; Lally, Barramundi fillets with a creamy herbed-lemon dressing.

'I'd like Chardonnay, please.' Lally felt pleased that her voice sounded normal. They'd opted out of the wine to start with, and she'd appreciated that too.

Cameron examined the labels of the wines the waiter had brought and approved a Chardonnay for Lally and a red for himself. The waiter poured and left, and they started their meals.

Cam answered her question then. 'The heroine would be doing her best to distract the hero and keep his mind jumping so he doesn't have time to wonder what she's up to.' He glanced at his plate and then hers. 'For us, for now, I'd like descriptions of the food so I can use the dishes in the book, I think. I can see the characters eating these meals.'

'Oh—okay. The fish is moist and flaky; the sauce is tart enough to balance the creaminess.' Lally did her best to describe the combination of textures and tastes.

She could see Cam making mental notes, and she tried to feel that they'd left behind their consciousness of each other, but it felt as though it still simmered beneath the surface.

There had to be some way to stop that simmering. It was inappropriate for her to simmer in this setting.

And if your boss is simmering?

Well, Lally didn't know—and what were they anyway, a matching set of human saucepans?

'Do you think you'll take on other property-development projects in Adelaide?' Yes, that was the way to express an everyday, businesslike interest and nothing more—ask a question that made her sound as though she wanted to be assured he wouldn't be leaving after a few short weeks!

'Tell me about your family. You mentioned art and restaurants.'

Cam spoke at the same time. They both stopped. He brushed his hand over the back of his neck.

If Lally got started on family, they would still be here when the place closed for the night. And she did want to know what his future plans might be, even if that made her nosy.

'I may take on further projects here.' Cam didn't seem to make too much of her question. He started to talk about other buildings in various parts of Adelaide. 'There's a block of apartments, dilapidated but in an area that I know would resell really well. I put an offer in on those earlier today.'

As though there was nothing exciting or fascinating about buying up another building; perhaps to him there wasn't. He bought and sold in dollar figures she could only dream about. She found his ability to write stories fascinating, too, his imagination and his interest in hands-on research. The dimple in his chin, the groove on his forehead...

Are not fascinating, Lally!

All right, fine; as a person, Cameron Travers was interesting—complex, busy, bordering on workaholic. And an insomniac. And, for whatever reason, Lally found all of this a little too intriguing for her own calm and controlled state of mind.

They made their way through the remainder of the meal. Cameron occasionally jotted notes on a small note-pad he drew from his trouser pocket, but Lally felt as though his attention never left her, never left *them.* Which was quite silly, because this wasn't about her or *them.*

Finally, they finished the last sip of their

coffee. Lally pushed away her half-eaten dessert of a profiterole filled with *crème* custard and coated in crunchy strands of caramelised sugar. 'That's delicious, but I can't fit it all in.'

Cam patted his flat stomach and pushed the platter of cheese and crackers into the middle of the table. 'I'm done there too.' He glanced at his watch and met her gaze with eyes that were piercing and interested, weary, alert and conscious of her all at once. 'It's after eleven. Will you come and do the final step of tonight's adventure with me now?'

Deep tone. Words meant to be about his work. Expression that was somewhat about that. Yet…

'That's what we're here for.' Lally agreed while her senses were in a muddle reacting to him.

She agreed before her brain engaged at all, really. That was dangerous, as was the feel of his arm holding her fingers tucked against his side as they left the restaurant after he paid for their meal. She could feel the muscles over his ribs moving as he walked; his skin beneath his shirt was warm against the back of her fingers.

He felt lean and fit—he *was* lean and fit—and

gorgeous and appealing into the bargain. Lally shouldn't be feeling these responses to him because she needed to protect herself. She was not ready to tackle another relationship with a man, and, even if she was, that man wasn't going to be a millionaire, incredibly focused, fabulous and famous temporary boss: Cam was way out of her league.

So, what was she about, leaning against his side this way?

They climbed into a service lift that took them to the top of the hotel.

'It's only five storeys high, but I do want to go all the way to the roof for this.' Cameron said it almost as though he felt he should apologise for this fact.

'Whatever works best for your story.' Lally told herself she had overcome her momentary lapse, that she had herself well in hand now.

That theory lasted until she looked into Cameron's eyes and her pulse started to throb at her wrists and at the base of her neck. And—oh, it was silly—she suddenly she felt a bit... nervous too.

'That's exactly what I wanted to see, Lally—the edge of caution, even though at this stage you don't believe you're in any true danger.' His words were a glide of consonants and cadence that crossed her senses like the brush of velvet over her skin. 'That's a look I can describe for my heroine to good effect in the book.'

The lift stopped and they stepped out onto the flat rooftop area of the building. Cam glanced around and led her towards the edge with a firm grip on her arm. 'You don't suffer from vertigo or anything like that?'

'No. I don't.' Even so, Lally made no bones about leaning into his firm hold now; it was a long drop to ground level. Too bad if that made her look clingy just at the moment. 'What?'

'Look at the drop for me. Then we're going to act out…' He led her close enough that she could look over.

As Lally truly registered that they stood five storeys up on a deserted rooftop late at night, her imagination kicked in. What did Cam plan to write about this setting? What did he want her to do?

Lally glanced at her boss, and adrenalin and

excitement coursed through her veins. It seemed necessary to speak in a hushed tone, and she whispered, 'This is going to be a real rush, isn't it? Like skydiving or something. My instincts are telling me it will be exciting. My heart's in my throat already and I don't even know yet.'

'I don't know what you'll think.' His fingers tightened their hold around her arm. 'But we're going to find out.'

CHAPTER SIX

'YOU'LL be completely safe, Lally, but you may not feel safe for a moment or two.' Cam's gaze searched her face.

'Whatever it is, I'm ready.' Lally ignored the breathless edge to her voice and the nervous tension that went with it.

Cam clasped his fingers loosely about her elbows. 'This would all happen very fast. She wouldn't have time to think, but for the point of this exercise I'll talk you through some of it. I want your thoughts on what her reactions would be.'

It was automatic for Lally's hands to come up and splay against his chest through the cloth of his dinner jacket. The evening bag was over one of her wrists. 'I think your heroine would feel her heart-rate speed up, and she would tell herself to be careful. Be very careful.'

Cameron's glance rested briefly on her mouth. 'She doesn't know whether he intends to kiss her, attack her, accuse her, hold her at gunpoint, try to overpower her or throw her over the edge. Is he on to her secrets?'

'And is she on to his?'

No sooner had Lally got the question out than Cam drew her back a little from the edge. He swept her up in his arms in a lightning-fast move. One hand came under the back of her thighs, the other cupped behind her shoulders. Her handbag was jammed between their bodies. His face was inches from hers.

They were a safe distance from the edge but, oh, it didn't feel safe in those first moments. Lally caught her breath and a soft gasp of sound left her parted lips. Her free hand locked around the back of his neck.

'Easy.' Cam felt Lally's arm lock around the muscles in his neck, and he took two long steps, not towards the edge but parallel to it. 'Sorry. I need to know how my male lead would feel carrying her.'

'If he's doing it to get closer to the edge, she'd be fighting him.' Lally's words brushed against his temple and cheek. 'She'd struggle to get free.'

Lally was tense, but not struggling.

Cam had to think about his characters. The research. He could see the characters clearly in his mind.

That was great; his instincts told him he would be able to write this scene. He had his female character fixed now, defined, he knew who she was and that she would work well for his story. That issue was resolved for Cam.

What wasn't resolved was his desire for the woman in his arms. That had been getting further and further away from his control since they'd first schemed this idea up earlier today. Maybe the excitement of it, the sheer fun of planning and executing it, was why Cam hadn't controlled his other responses to Lally very well.

'Yes, she would struggle to get free, but I'll deal with working that out for myself or we can role-play it elsewhere. Even though we're away from the edge, I don't want to risk losing my balance or anything while we're up here.' He tried to sound focused and interested in the research. Not distracted…

'If he does intend to throw her, the best thing she could do is refuse to release her hold on him, unless he was prepared to go over with her.' Lally made this observation with what judiciousness she could find in the face of her distraction. Being held this way, held close to Cam's broad chest, made thinking difficult. 'Or unless he had the capacity to subdue her some other way before he tossed her over.'

In tandem with her words, Lally's hand locked harder about his neck.

Cam moved his body enough to allow her to get her other hand free. 'In the scene, she would struggle to get that hand loose.'

Lally added it to her hold about his neck. 'So she'd hold on like this?'

'At this stage, yes.' God, his voice was way too deep, and his entire body seemed utterly focused on what he held.

And what he held was Lally Douglas in a flowing, beautiful dress that made her look both sultry and alluring. He felt the brush of the soft fabric over his hand where he held her in his arms; the hem wrapped around his trouser legs. He held Lally, her face upturned towards his, excitement and an edge of uncertainty stamped on that face.

It was not because she didn't feel safe with him. There was apprehension of another kind, the sort a person felt when they entered uncharted territory with someone they found attractive.

Are you cataloguing her reactions now, Travers, or your reactions to her?

Cam stopped walking and murmured, 'She would quite probably try to reach for the gun in her purse.'

'Yes.' Her words whispered into the stillness. She didn't move.

Cam's focus was on her face, his gaze touching on each feature—eyes, cheeks, nose, finally lingering on her mouth. His look, filled with want, desire and something perhaps deeper than both of those things, drew Lally's gaze to his eyes and locked it there. Her breath stilled all over again. All around them was darkness and city silence, which was no silence at all, but it still shrouded them in isolation here while the world went by below.

Darkness and aloneness and consciousness.

Cam's gaze met hers once more in the dimness, and everything slid into a different place for Lally. The evening; the slow meal and their talk about his writing and work projects; her determination not to look too deeply into herself: it had all mixed in together and blurred into this one moment that was so much more than the compilation of those parts. That really had nothing at all to do with those parts.

'I shouldn't have picked you up like this.' He murmured the words, but he didn't let her go.

Instead his hand wrapped more firmly behind her shoulders and he shifted to stand with his legs splayed apart.

His head lowered towards her. 'Tell me not to…'

'Not to…?' But Lally knew. She looked into his eyes and she couldn't say the words. How could she say those words to Cam when his gaze was on her this way, desire stamped across his cheekbones, burned into the shadows beneath his eyes, etched over lips that softened and dipped towards hers?

She should say no. She needed to protect her emotions and not take risks, but Lally could only wait while her lips softened in anticipation.

And then he was there. The kiss she had secretly longed for was happening.

His lips tasted faintly of coffee, and were both firm and gentle as he softly kissed her, oh, so softly, as though they had all the time in the world and all he wanted to do was this.

She'd thought she was holding her own, that she had control over this evening with him. That she had at least held on to a little of what it was all about, remembered they were doing this for his research and no other reason.

Well, this didn't feel like research. Her lips softened beneath his and when he slid her slowly down his body until her feet touched concrete it felt natural and right to let his arms close around her, to step fully into his embrace and let the kiss take them where it would.

Cam made a soft sound in the back of his

throat. He deepened their kiss, his lips caress-
ing hers, moulding to hers, tasting and giving
and taking. One hand splayed against the small
of her back; the long, lean fingers of the other
wrapped around her jaw.

Lally responded with a deepening of desire for
him, but she also softened for him. Her emotions
melted into a puddle inside her; if he'd wanted,
he could have walked straight in and…

Well, she wasn't sure. Taken whatever he
wanted? Hurt her because she wasn't ready to
trust a man again, wasn't sure she could ever do
that again? She wasn't sure she could trust herself.

Lally became conscious of just how intimately
they were pressed together; their bodies were
flush against each other from chest to knee.
Cam's fingers were stroking up and down her
bare shoulders and back. Hers—were in his hair,
clasping his shoulder while her entire body
seemed to strain for closeness with his.

Oh, Lally. What are you thinking?

Lally forced her mouth to leave his, her body
to draw back. Each action felt as though it took
an aeon to execute. She shouldn't feel *anything*

towards Cam, not in this way. He was her boss; she was his employee. Lally felt panicked.

Think how Cam kissed you, Lally. How he drew a response from you so easily and so thoroughly, made you feel as though you were receiving your first ever real kiss.

Sam had made her feel that way. With Sam, it *had* been her first ever kiss. First kiss, first everything.

That was hardly the point here.

Well, what was the point? She couldn't let herself be affected by what they had shared in these moments. She couldn't let herself care again—

Lally forced herself to meet Cam's gaze and opened her mouth to speak, to play this down, to say something about work or characterisation or research.

Anything.

But her lips still tingled from the press of his. Even now her body begged her to step back into his embrace, to take their kiss even further, prolong the closeness and connection.

Finally Lally found words. 'I'm not looking

for an involvement. Not that I'm suggesting you
are. This… We forgot ourselves for a moment.
There's no need to make a fuss about it, but it
mustn't happen again; it's not wise. You're a
busy man with loads on your plate, and your
struggle to sleep to deal with, let alone a recal-
citrant muse and a highly demanding business
in Sydney. And I work for you!'

'I know.' He swallowed hard. Regret etched
lines into his face that hadn't been there before.
'I understand all of that, Lally. It was wrong of
me to kiss you. I'm not looking for a relationship. I don't—that's not in my agenda, and it's
not smart to mix work with that anyway. And
you're quite right. You wouldn't want…'

Whatever he'd been about to say, he cut the
words off, but the message was there anyway.
He agreed with her. This kiss shouldn't have
happened. They had to respect the boundaries
of their working relationship. He didn't want
her, not really. Not like that.

Lally drew a breath and blurted, 'I didn't mean
to set up this night to lead to this.'

'I know.' His words were deep and genuine.

'I had a problem with my writing, you thought of a great solution. We both got excited about it and in that excitement, for a few moments, we forgot ourselves.'

His summary of events left out a few things—such as the way they'd both become more aware of each other as the evening had worn on—but Lally nodded. 'That's right. I'm glad we got that sorted out.' She forced a relieved smile. 'Phew. Well, are we finished here? Do you have what you need for your research? Maybe we should head home—I mean, back to your property development.'

'I have everything I need.' Cam watched emotions flit across Lally's face and felt them churn inside him. Kissing her had been amazing. Yes, he'd made all sorts of comments on how that had come about and why it shouldn't have and everything else. Those comments were real and true; they just weren't all of it. And they didn't even begin to touch on how he'd felt inside himself as a result of these shared moments. Cam didn't want to examine those feelings, but the thoughts came anyway.

He'd kissed her softly in a way he had never kissed any other woman. He'd kissed Lally after trying to ignore the need to do it all night. He'd kissed her to pay homage to her beauty and how lovely she looked in that dress. He'd done it because something inside him had needed to.

He couldn't tell her any of that. Because Lally didn't want this. She'd made that clear and she'd looked scared when she said it. Scared from somewhere inside that Cam shouldn't mess with because she could end up getting hurt, and the last thing he wanted was to hurt her.

He wanted to know *what* had hurt her, but he mustn't mess with that either. He had no right, no claim on her, aside from being her very temporary employer, nor would he ever seek to change that. Cam didn't want this either; he couldn't pursue it. He'd only end up disappointing her, not being what she needed. He'd proved that about himself already.

He was an insomniac, workaholic, novel-writing businessman who couldn't stay in one place, couldn't rest, had no idea how to be a family. He and his mother might have been linked during his childhood but she hadn't wanted him. And Cam had learned not to be wanted.

He'd tried to break out of that once, in his mid-twenties. Gillian…

Cam had built up Gillian's expectations, and when she'd realised just how much of him would never be hers, when she had come to understand just how much his past history and his insomnia impacted on his daily life, she'd been let down, disappointed and ultimately hurt. She'd wanted and needed more than he'd been able to give her. She'd been right to want that, and right to walk away.

They'd gone their separate ways and Cam had learned a lesson. He didn't want to hurt a woman like that again. He didn't want to set himself up for that kind of loss again either. He knew what he could and couldn't have.

Yet tonight Cam had forgotten all that past history, that painful learning-curve that he'd sworn not to repeat. He'd kissed a slip of a girl on a rooftop, had found all this tenderness and all these other responses to her inside him. He hadn't simply wanted to give them to her, he'd felt *driven* to bring them to her. That wasn't something he'd experienced with Gillian; it wasn't something he'd ever experienced with any woman.

That fact perhaps had driven him to kiss Lally. It had certainly made his reactions to her even more dangerous. He forced his arms to drop away from her, forced himself to take a step back. Every fibre of his body and mind seemed to object at once. If he drew her close again, he knew he wouldn't want to let go at all. He'd take her hand, lead her back through this hotel, take her home and make her his completely.

Not happening, Travers.

'We should go.' He led Lally back the way they had come and ushered her into the service lift.

As the doors closed, Lally turned to him and said quietly, 'Your book—did we achieve what you needed?'

It was a ploy to get the focus off them and back to the reason for this evening. Cam acknowledged this and did his best to further it. 'I've decided the female character will be an undercover special-services officer, but she's a double agent with marksman skills and a history as a hired assassin as well…' Cam talked about his story until he had Lally out of the hotel and safely ensconced beside him in the car.

In the car's dim interior, Cam could hear every breath Lally took, smell the soft scent of her skin and whatever lotion she'd rubbed into it after her shower tonight. He tried not to notice any of it.

'I'm glad the research was successful and that you have a good understanding of this new character you're bringing into your story.' Her fingers fidgeted with the small bag in her lap. 'You know, I really shouldn't keep any of these things.'

'Please. Maybe you'll wear them some place again one day.' *And think of me.* Was that what Cam wanted? His eyebrows drew together.

As they passed beneath a streetlight, Cam glanced towards her. The breeze had whipped at her hair, dishevelled it just enough to make him want to bury his hands in it, caress his fingers over her scalp and use that touch to tilt her head so he could kiss her neck, kiss her chin and find his way back to soft lips.

You're not thinking about kissing her, remember?

They'd researched; that research had led to a kiss that shouldn't have happened. A kiss that had blown him away, because she'd been so giving and he'd loved that and had wanted to give back in equal measure. Cam drew the convertible to a halt in an allotted space inside the property-development site. No matter how tempting, no matter how much she soothed him—no matter anything—he had to take due care that nothing like this happened again.

A woman like Lally deserved better than an insomniac workaholic who had no sense of family or ability to meet a woman's deep needs.

There was no other way for Cam. No other way that he knew.

CHAPTER SEVEN

'HE PUSHES himself so hard, Auntie. I really want to help him find a way to get more sleep. It's the one thing I think I might be able to do for him, beyond the work I'm already doing.'

A week had passed since the night Lally and Cam had role-played, when he had tried to 'toss her over' the top of the hotel.

Lally had revisited those moments more often than she wanted to admit—not the pretend tossing, but the kissing that hadn't been about role-playing at all.

Cam had placed his lips over hers and it had felt like the sweetest kiss of all time, sweet and gentle and tender, and Lally needed to forget it. She must have built it way up in her mind, anyway, mustn't she? For how could she feel such a depth of reaction and response to something that, for him, must only have been the result of place, time and circumstance, nothing more?

She couldn't start to have feelings about Cam, or towards Cam, not like those.

Lally bit back a sigh. 'He's my *employer.*' She put a certain emphasis on the word 'employer'; yes, that drew even more attention to her need to hold him to that role in her thinking.

If she thought of him in that light, spoke of him in that light, then eventually she would accept he *was* only in that light for her.

Lally glanced about her. It was only just past dawn, but already the markets were teeming with life. Mum stood with her arm linked through Aunt Edie's. Well, that was family; you all looked after each other.

Lally felt a sudden tug of emotion as she acknowledged that thought. For six years she'd built her life around looking after everyone as best she could, and then they hadn't needed her.

'I've missed everyone. You didn't mention how Jodie is getting along. How could I not ask about one of my sisters? Thanks for meeting me here this morning for coffee and talking about so many of them.' She'd asked them to come and had used wanting to help her boss as her reason. And that *had* been the reason. Mostly.

They'd talked. Mum and Auntie had brought her up to speed on all the gossip about the family—well, almost all. Lally reiterated that she could take calls and text messages at work, that her boss wouldn't mind.

Mum and Auntie seemed fine about that, but Lally still came away from that part of the conversation wondering if there was more under the surface. Maybe she should have just asked, but a part of her was scared of the possible answer.

Perhaps the issues with her employer were behind her general sense of unease. He'd done an exemplary job of avoiding her in the past week, aside from meal times, handing over work-lists and asking her to do various specific jobs for him. Another research trip had needed two sets of hands, not one.

He hasn't avoided you at all, Latitia. You've seen loads of him.

Lally frowned. That was right, she had seen

loads of him, so why did she almost feel as though she was missing him?

'Jodie's fine,' Mum said.

Lally bit her lip. 'Good. I'm glad.' She was. And, if the answer to her other question was that she wanted Cam all over her with gentle feelings, and maybe the need to kiss her again, then she needed to stop longing for things that were completely out of the question. She was better off without them, because she really wasn't ready to face that kind of emotional gymnastics again.

You don't deserve ever to have a meaningful fulfilling relationship. Not after all the harm you've caused in the past.

The thought sent a shaft of pain through Lally's chest. 'What were we talking about?'

'You were telling us about your hunky new employer,' Auntie declared, and a grin split her weathered brown face.

'My boss has insomnia,' Lally said primly, and in a depressing tone focused on stopping Auntie's speculations. 'I woke three times last night, and every time I could see a strip of light beneath his office door and knew he was in there, working.'

Lally had been restless; she'd been restless ever since the night he'd kissed her, to be honest. 'I wanted to know about bush foods and remedies for Cam in case there might be something that would help him sleep better.'

Her voice softened when she said his name; it went completely to mush just like that. And, because that was such a give away, Lally felt a blush build beneath her skin. She needed to put Auntie and Mum off the scent, not encourage more speculation.

'Fresh food is a good start, of course.' Auntie spoke as she examined Lally's face.

'For Cam, yes.' Mum chipped in with her opinion, and a gleam in her eyes that definitely seemed to hold a hint of satisfaction.

Could the family have conspired to get Lally out into the world, as she'd wondered, with a view to her meeting a man, maybe?

Lally glanced at her watch and found a sudden need to become highly time-efficient. 'I should get on with my shopping while we finish this talk.' Lally strode to the nearest fruit stall and lifted a ripe pawpaw. If this also happened to mean that she wasn't quite so obviously the centre of their speculation, well, that was purely happenstance.

Mum and Auntie quickly caught up with her, and Lally decided, if they were talking, she might as well spit out something else that she'd avoided once already this morning. It was bothering her. She was better off dealing with it so it could stop doing so.

Lally turned. 'This job is the first one I've had where I wasn't working for family. I want to do well at this, but I also need to know I'll be coming back to the family the minute my work is done for Cameron Travers. Someone will need me, won't they?'

'Oh, well, I'm sure they will, but haven't you found spreading your wings to be fun? It sounds as though it has been.' Mum went on, 'You say your employer bought you a dress and a handbag, and you helped him with research on the roof of a hotel at midnight?'

Well, not at midnight, but Lally supposed that was near enough. And, yes, it had been exciting. It just had also become somewhat complicated by the end of the night. 'Yes, we did some research for his current book.' Lally paid for the pawpaw and set it gently into the bottom of her shopping basket. 'But, truly, the only reason I brought up his name this morning is because I want to try to help him sleep better. He looks so exhausted.' She turned to her aunt. 'Do you have any ideas?'

Auntie's wrinkled face creased into even deeper lines. 'There *are* bush foods and remedies; it depends on why he's that way in the first place. Has he seen a doctor?'

'I asked him about that the other day. He's visited doctors and sleep specialists, done all the sleep studies. I think he's tried everything he's been told to try and come to the end of the line with no real solutions.' Lally hesitated. 'It's not that he's not alert, because he always is—he's sharp as a whip—it's just that…'

'He's sharp while he's pushing himself, can't relax, only sleeps until the edge is off his exhaustion, then he wakes and it's on again for another day for him.' Auntie nodded.

She transferred her hold from Mum's arm to

Lally's and they made their way through the remaining market-stalls. Lally worked through her shopping list while Auntie talked.

'You remember the tribal elder I took you to visit when you were a girl?' Auntie named the elder. 'He has a store. He and his wife know just about all there is to know about this kind of thing. It might be worth giving them a call.'

Lally did remember, and wished she'd thought of this earlier. 'Thanks. That's exactly what I need.'

They completed the shopping. 'Thanks for meeting me this morning. I should get back to work.'

Mum laid her hand on Lally's arm. 'If you're interested in your boss…'

Yes, there was definitely a gleam in Mum's eyes that said 'the plan is working.' Auntie's too.

Lally's mouth formed words before she could stop them. 'You all ganged together to say there was no work so I'd get out more, didn't you?'

She wanted to be angry, to say 'how could you?'

But Mum gave a sheepish nod and came right

out and admitted it. 'We wanted you to have some fun, Lally. Maybe this boss…'

'He kissed me and I kissed him back, but it was a bad idea on both our parts and neither of us wants it.' Lally drew a breath. Apparently her mother still possessed the ability to get her to confess, even when it should have been Mum doing the confessing. 'I just care about his insomnia issues. It's in my nature to care. I've always cared about the family.'

Lally gave Mum a stern stare. 'Even when they've tossed me out on some made-up pretext without so much as a by your leave.'

'The family cares about you, Lally.' Mum sighed. 'Please don't be angry. Maybe we shouldn't have done that, but it's only for two months. We wanted to help, to see you enjoy yourself, maybe just make some nice friends.'

'Or meet a man friend?' Lally shook her head. 'I wish you hadn't. You don't understand.' But she wasn't mad, and she gave Mum a hug to make that clear. 'It's too late to change anything now, but I'd appreciate it if you all didn't do this again.'

'We interfered too much. I'm sorry, Lally.' Mum looked guilt-ridden.

Lally let it go. 'It's okay.' She gave a wry smile. 'In a family the size of ours, interfering happens. I know that.' Lally couldn't explain why she didn't want a man in her life again. She bit her lip.

Auntie had wandered a little distance while Lally and Mum talked. She returned now and glanced at her watch. 'Are you ready to go, Susan?'

'Indeed I am.' Mum gave Lally another hug.

Auntie gave Lally a hug.

Lally hugged both of them back, and then there were more quick words and waves. There was no need to say anything to Auntie about the rest of it.

They disappeared, and Lally walked towards the exit of the market. It was only a few blocks back to her boss's development; maybe the walk would help her to clear her mind. At least she knew what her family had been up to now. They'd better all start contacting her again, or she *would* have something to say about that!

Lally glanced into her basket, checked the contents one last time and realised she'd forgotten the baby-spinach leaves she'd wanted to use in a warm chicken salad for lunch. She turned around and strode back into the heart of the market again.

'Lally, wait up, I'll carry the basket for you.' It was Cam's voice, morning-roughened and deep.

He'd called from behind her; Lally turned her head and looked over her shoulder and there he was, his gaze fixed on her as he strode forward through the crowd.

Her heart did a ridiculous lift. The world seemed suddenly brighter simply because she'd caught a glance of his face, a glimpse of a smile and softened expression directed her way.

Oh, Lally, can't you do better than that at resisting how he makes you feel? Do you want to end up out of your depth again? He's already made it clear he isn't interested.

Lally just couldn't trust again. The risks were too big. So she had to focus on the ways she could be a good employee to him.

As he joined her, Lally examined his face for

signs of weariness—she found them. 'You couldn't sleep again this morning?'

'No, and I'm sorry if I disturbed you last night.' He scrubbed a hand over his jaw; it bore a day's beard-growth. That combined with a pair of jeans, black T-shirt, and shades pushed up on his head, looked just a little disreputable. Appealingly so.

Not noticing, Lally!

She said quickly, 'You didn't disturb me. I was already awake. I'm just sorry you haven't been managing to sleep more.'

'That's how it is.' He took her arm and raised his eyebrows. 'Where are you headed? When I first spotted you, I thought you'd finished and were ready to go home.'

He'd walked here just to meet her, to carry the basket for her; Lally handed it over and Cam held it easily in one hand.

She drew a breath. 'I forgot to get baby spinach. I want it for our lunch.' Healthy foods, healthy ingredients; she would try to help Cam eat well and sleep better. She had to try. 'Have you had a check-up lately for your insomnia?

There might be new treatments. I meant to ask that when we discussed this the other day.'

'I have check-ups a couple of times a year.' He shrugged his shoulders. 'So far, permanently fixing it for me hasn't worked out. I know it's not something people can put up with.'

Now, what did he mean by that?

'Let's get the spinach. Over there?' He waited while she made her purchase, and then walked with her back to the exit. They walked through and started back home along the suburban streets.

Lally had to stop thinking of it as home. It wasn't even particularly home-like; the project was going to be full of rental apartments, for goodness' sake, and Cam wouldn't even be staying here once the work was done. Just because she'd become used to thinking of all sorts of places among her family as home didn't mean she could add Cam's property-development project to that list.

Lally didn't know what he'd meant about people not putting up with his insomnia, but was the answer all that relevant? She could try to help him, that was all.

'I met my mother and aunt here this morning

and asked Auntie about folklore. Changes in diet and some bush remedies may help—they won't harm you, and I'd like to try.'

'You're welcome to do that.' It was clear he meant it. 'It's thoughtful of you.'

Lally's heart did an odd little stutter. 'I'm happy to do that.' *Don't let yourself be too happy with him, Lally. It's dangerous.*

But she turned her face up to the sun and felt happiness get her anyway. 'I think it's going to be quite hot later today.'

'Yes, help yourself to a swim in the pool if you want to. It's safe to swim in now.' He led her around a child's tricycle that had been left abandoned on the footpath. 'I swam in it myself this morning before I came out to find you. The water's the perfect temperature, thanks to the pool's heating.'

'I brought a swimsuit; I might take a dip some time. We could—I mean *I*...' Lally cut herself off quickly before she could say more. What she definitely must not do was let her mind wander to swimming in that pool with her employer.

At midnight, when it was quiet and silent and

they had complete privacy to bathe by moon-light, or at least by city light. Either way would be quite romantic.

Which ruled the idea out entirely!

As for her happiness, that stemmed from no longer feeling uneasy about her work future, or her family.

Yes. It was all about that.

Cameron watched the changes of expression cross Lally's face, watched interest and attraction to him war with good sense.

Lally had met with her mother and aunt at least in some part for his sake. Cam couldn't remember the last time anyone had done something to try to care for him. He couldn't remember that ever happening. His mother hadn't exactly been the type, and he'd gone out on his own the first chance he'd got anyway.

Nowadays his mother just gave in to her wandering gene completely and went wherever the mood took her without ever making even a half-hearted effort to convince herself to try to settle anywhere.

Most of the time he wouldn't have been able to track her down if he'd wanted to. The thing was he pretty much didn't want to any more.

Whatever missing gene his mother lacked when it came to family had passed squarely down to Cam. He'd got over trying to connect with her.

Yet he would have liked to meet some of Lally's family.

'I'm sorry I missed meeting your mother and aunt.' Cam tucked her hand more securely against his side. 'And thank you for wanting to help with my sleep issues. Having you around to do some of the day-to-day things is a help all by itself, whether I'm sleeping more as a result or not.'

He turned his head to smile down into her upturned face. Had he gone about with blinkers on until now to stop himself from truly noticing loveliness? Because Lally was lovely in ways he hadn't seen before in anyone else. Beautiful, oh yes, she was that—but her beauty came from inside her as well as from her looks. He'd wanted—no, needed—to dress her in that vibrant outfit last week to pay homage to that beauty, to see it shine, and let all the world see it shine.

The night might have started out as an attempt at trying to rattle his muse loose, and Cam was grateful that that had indeed happened and he'd made good progress with his book since then. But he'd taken pleasure in Lally from the outset that evening. He forced himself to admit this.

Lally had shone. Her eyes had glowed, and she'd chosen the sexiest pair of high heels and worn them as though she'd been made to wear such things. Cam had wanted to sweep her up and kiss her senseless.

He'd done exactly that, and come out of it feeling as if he'd been the one swept off his feet at the top of that building. He hadn't been able to get their kiss out of his mind since. For the first time in his life, Cam was faced with a particular dilemma that he hadn't faced before: he wanted something that he knew he couldn't have, and he couldn't seem to get past the depth of that wanting. He wanted that closeness with Lally again, wanted to be able to take it forward, but he wasn't capable of successfully doing that, and he knew it.

'Auntie knows a lot of bush lore, remedies from our people that might help you.' Lally's eyes had softened and mellowed into warm, sherry pools.

Cam noted that, noted the sting of deeper colour across her cheekbones, and felt the skin of his face tighten in response. Did she know he could see her awareness, her interest, even as she did all she could to fight it? She was trying to stick to the topic of helping him somehow, and even that was way too sweet of her. But her expression also gave away other feelings.

Cam shouldn't want to see that…

Lally's gaze locked with Cam's and for a long moment she didn't breathe. Her body distilled into consciousness of Cam even as they walked the final stretch of footpath and began to hear the sounds of construction, men calling to each other, hammers, drills and pieces of timber being lifted and dropped.

Her gaze shifted to a point just below Cam's chin. 'I won't try any quack remedies on you, in case you're worried. Auntie would never recommend anything dangerous, or suggest I consult with anyone who would. I know I can trust her judgement with that.'

'What does your aunt do for a living? Or is she retirement age?' Cam asked the question to force his thoughts away from wanting to take her into his arms, but he realised he was truly interested. In fact, he admitted he had been intrigued and interested in Lally's history from the day they'd met. He'd put that down to the curiosity of his writer's mind, but he had to admit this felt more personal. He wanted to *know* Lally, know her deeply, understand what made her tick.

Cam had needed to figure out the female character for his book. Lally had helped him with that.

But the need to know *Lally,* to understand her, that was something that still burned in Cam.

'My aunt is an artist and a potter.' A hint of pride crept into Lally's voice. 'Her pottery and clay sculptures are truly unique and very beautiful. She's fifty-five but I don't think she has any plans to stop working on her art any time soon.'

'Your family seems to have a lot of talent between them.' Cam's words held admiration.

'I think so. I'm very proud of them.' Lally waited while Cam walked them through the courtyard area and into his apartment.

And then she did what she needed to do, and had to keep doing until it became her habit, her 'this is how it is and will go on being' self.

'Thank you for carrying the produce for me. If you have anything new for my duties list, please jot it down and leave it on the kitchen bench for me. I'm going to start some laundry and then I'll be back to prepare breakfast. I'm sure you'll be very busy, so I'll make sure I keep out of your way.'

Without looking at Cam's face, Lally removed herself to the laundry and buried her thoughts in the process of sorting the fluffies from the non-fluffies.

That was what housekeepers did—and her work was *all* Lally should focus on doing!

CHAPTER EIGHT

'I WISH I could figure out what's missing from the courtyard area.' Cam had just come from a phone call that Lally had asked him to take and had walked into the kitchen to return the mobile phone to her.

The call had been about an issue happening at his Sydney firm, and he'd resolved it easily enough. When he rejoined Lally in the kitchen, his gaze had shifted to the courtyard, and he'd again been struck by the thought that something was missing out there. 'I've already discussed with the site boss making the courtyard a feature area in the complex. He's advised against it. He feels that smaller, separate outdoor-areas would be the way to go. But people might want to be able to mingle.'

'It could turn into a real little community, almost like a family,' Lally said.

'Can you spare a minute, Mr Travers?' The site boss spoke as he knocked on the open apartment-door. 'Those door panels we ordered have arrived. I think they'll do as a substitute for the ones you originally wanted that were out of stock, but I figured you'd want to see for yourself.'

Cam did want to see. Lally was already turning away to start her lunch preparations.

'I'll come now.' Cam stepped outside and told himself it was perhaps best that they'd been interrupted. What was the point of plying Lally with personal questions that couldn't make any difference to their relationship anyway?

That would be the relationship you're not having with her—the one that involves not thinking about kissing her, not wanting to kiss her again and not needing to know everything about her and understand her even more?

Lally Douglas was his housekeeper and assistant. He didn't need to know her past and her history and what made her tick. *He didn't.*

Cam's mobile phone beeped in his pocket and

he made a mental note to check his text messages straight after this. Somehow, multi-tasking every moment of his day didn't feel quite as appealing any more.

When had that happened to him?

'Right. Let's look at these panels.' He strode purposefully forward with the site boss. At least his writing and the development were going well.

Two evenings later, Cam and Lally stood in the swimming pool with their arms resting on the edge. It was Friday, around eight p.m. The day had been unseasonably hot, and they'd both made their way to the pool to cool off. Cam had already been in the water doing laps when Lally had joined him.

They'd swum, and Cam had told himself not to think about long, bare limbs and a flow of wet hair down the graceful curve of her back. Now they were side by side in the water at the edge of the pool, looking out over the courtyard. Lally wore a one-piece teal swimsuit. It was modest, not that Cam should be giving more than a cursory glance anyway.

'I'd put a pebble mosaic there.' Lally raised one wet arm to point her finger at the centre of the courtyard. 'One with a water feature in the middle so it made the area feel cool and restful all year round. I'd do it in earth tones and use a style similar to a dot-work motif.'

'Symbolic of a traditional Aboriginal painting?' Cam forced his thoughts to that idea. 'That would look good. The colours would work with the existing pavers. The fact that they're weathered would work really well with it. Do you know much about that kind of work?'

Cam turned his head to look at her, and came very close to totally losing his train of thought.

Lally was in the process of wringing the excess water out of her hair. The swimsuit *was* modest—one-piece, cut to her thighs, criss-crossing over her breasts and coming up into a halter tie at the back of her neck—but the outfit also left rather a lot of her back bare to his gaze. Her shoulders were gently sloped, fine-boned and sun-kissed. Cam wanted to follow where the sun had been, kissing his way to where she'd lifted her hair to wring it out and tie it in a loose knot at the back of her head.

Sleek, touchable hair that looked different with some of the curl soaked out of it.

No touching, no thinking about touching, and definitely no memory of kissing or wanting to do it again.

'I've done mosaics myself.' Lally uttered the words in a voice that held an edge of breathlessness, but not because of the topic of conversation. Her gaze dipped to his bare chest and skittered away again. That simply, that easily, they were back to where they'd been all those nights ago when he'd held her in his arms at the top of that building.

Cam had tried not to let his thoughts return there. He tried now, but he couldn't tear his eyes from her—from every feature, every curve and dip, and all the loveliness from her soft, brown eyes to the lips that he had tasted and dreamed of tasting again. 'Lally?'

'I'd make a circular theme for the mosaic.' Lally pushed the words out as Cam leaned towards her, and she leaned towards him.

'That sounds good.' It did, but looking into her eyes felt better. Stupid, maybe, but better.

'With…' Lally stopped and drew a deep breath. 'With a pathway leading to the water feature and leading away from it. The feature itself would be at the centre of the circles.'

Cam's hand rose; his fingers just brushed across her damp shoulder. He wanted to pull her against his chest and kiss her until he was satisfied by the taste of her, the velvet of her mouth, the press of her softness against him. Instead, he nodded. 'With the right colours and design, that could be really striking. Restful and interesting at the same time.'

Cam cleared his throat and discovered his hand had come to rest on the pool-edging beside her. Though he wasn't touching her at all, his body formed a half-cradle around hers. She could shift away in an instant, or she could take that one movement forward, all the way into his arms.

'That's what I thought.' Her words were as distracted and breathless as his had been deep. She seemed to force herself to stick to the topic. 'There's a lot of garden edging the courtyard area—predominantly green most of the year, I'm guessing, with a few assorted colours of flowers? I think a mosaic in traditional colours from white sand through to ochre and dark browns would work really well.'

'Yes.' Cam inhaled and didn't think about her mouth. Not at all. 'And the mosaic itself could tell a story, couldn't it?'

'It could. The stones in the centre, surrounding the water feature, could represent a lake or the sea.' She drew a shaky breath. 'Coming in and going out of the feature could be rivers surrounded by their sandy banks.'

'Right.' Cam's mind worked through the idea slowly at first, but he liked it. 'Will you do it for me, Lally?'

Before she lowered her gaze, he thought that she had murmured she would do anything for him.

When she lifted her head, her shoulders were thrown back and she had a glint of determination in her eyes, a businesslike determination. 'You should know I've only done a couple of smaller mosaics in the past, but I do have confidence that—with the help of the site boss to guide me with the water-feature part of it—I could do a good job of this.'

If Lally said she could do it, she could do it. 'We'd need to make some trips to beaches to gather the colours of pebbles you want.'

'I'd thought to perhaps source the pebbles industrially, but gathering them straight off beaches would mean more interesting stones.' Lally nodded. 'They would definitely give the mosaic a more natural look and feel.'

'You didn't tell me you're an artist like some of the others in your family.' One of her referees had noted that Lally should be painting—was she capable of that too?

Lally moved away from him finally and made her way to the steps. She grasped the railing with one hand and looked at him over her shoulder. He could almost believe that those earlier moments hadn't happened. Almost.

'I haven't done much painting.' Lally went on. 'More than one family member has encouraged me to really take it on, and I would like to learn. It's a privilege to be handed down painting traditions and stories within the family. I don't know why I've put it off.' Yet shadows filled her eyes as she admitted she'd stalled on pursuing this part of her life.

'What's in your past, Lally Douglas?' What was there to make her feel she couldn't let herself have that privilege she'd just described? Had she held herself back from painting, just as she'd held back from allowing herself to bloom with all the vibrancy and colour she should embrace in other ways? What would make her feel that way?

'Nothing. There's nothing,' she uttered.

Cam wrapped a towel around his waist while she dried off in jerky movements and tied her towel sarong-style with a knot between her breasts. The words had come out too quickly, too defensively.

Their eyes met and locked, and Cam sensed so much hurt.

'I didn't mean to pry.' His gaze softened on her taut face, the tight shoulders and defensive posture. He wanted to cuddle her, to pull her gently into his arms, to wrap his hold right around her and encourage her to feel completely safe, unthreatened and secure.

Cam wanted to protect Lally, because there

was something. That fact was now abundantly clear. Cam thought it might have been a man.

The thought of some nameless male hurting Lally was hard for Cam to take. He didn't want to think of anyone doing that to her.

So don't you mess with her, Travers. You can't give her those gentle, kind things you just thought about. You might have had a random thought about them, but they're not for you to give to her. Don't hurt her by pulling her into anything when you can't follow it through.

If Cam drew Lally close, he would end up hurting her.

So he looked away, and Lally looked away.

She said with a great attempt at brightness, 'The garden would play its part to make a pebble mosaic look great. The two things would complement each other. There's already potential in the garden; it's overgrown and untended but the basics are there.'

She stepped across the courtyard to the nearest part of the garden and tugged a leaf from a mint plant. When she rubbed the leaf between her fingers, the pungent smell of the mint released into the air. 'The mosaic would boost the garden, and the garden would enhance the mosaic.'

'You're completely right. I wanted a solution for this area, and what you've suggested works.'

Lally had said it would make the area feel welcoming, and she'd mentioned giving a sense of community, like a family. If Cam wanted that…

He wanted it for his prospective tenants, even if the site boss recommended otherwise.

And when it came to his responses to Lally, his consciousness of her, yes, Cam still felt the tug of desire, the war of emotions he didn't understand. He also felt the ongoing impact of gut-deep weariness.

He didn't notice that as often when he was in her company. And he felt Lally's secrets, whatever they were. He had his, too, and these facts just underlined the importance of keeping an employer-employee line in the metaphorical sand between them.

For both their sakes, for so many reasons.

'My mother asked me to travel to a place on the coast to see her.' Cam's text messages had told him this; now he put it together with the thought of Lally creating this mosaic. 'She's going to be there tomorrow and invited me to have dinner with her. The town she'll be in is out of the way, slow roads for some of it, but there are a lot of good beaches around that area.'

Cam kept his mother informed of his whereabouts. She usually failed to respond to any of that information, but now and again they managed a meeting. It was usually Cam who went looking for those, though he didn't look all that often.

'That'll be nice for you, but perhaps a bit of a strain with the trip itself.' Lally made this comment as she absorbed her employer's statement that he planned to see his mother. 'You'll take care on the roads? Not drive if you're too tired?'

Lally wanted the meeting to be great for Cam. She'd thought he and his mum would be close, but he'd said they didn't see each other often. And his tone of voice as he'd said that…?

'Would you like to make a combined trip of it? We can scour up and down some beaches in that area for pebbles.' Cam's words interrupted her thoughts. 'I wouldn't anticipate us being with my mother for more than a couple of hours. We could squeeze in scouring one beach, maybe, before we meet her tomorrow. Stay overnight somewhere, look at some more beaches the following day, early, then head back here? I'd really like you to do this work, Lally. If you're willing.'

'I would like to do it.' Oh, Lally would like it very much. But an overnight stay away with him?

She told herself this was about practicalities, about getting materials, and it *was* about that. He'd asked about her past, but that wasn't relevant to this. It didn't come into making a mosaic, or attending dinner with he and his mother. Or anything.

'I think I'd really like you to meet my mother.' Cam murmured the words and then seemed surprised by them.

Lally was, too, and then it hit her that she would be meeting her boss's only relative. Whether it turned out they were close or not, what would his mother think of her? Lally wanted to make a good impression.

'I have to figure out what to wear,' she blurted, and blushed with fiery heat beneath her skin. Yes, she needed to make a good impression, but only as his employee. 'Um, I mean, I'd like to know where we'll be meeting her. Will it be a casual sort of place, or more formal? Because I can do either, but not in that dress we bought for your research. That would be way too much.'

As was her mega-blabbing!

Lally closed her teeth together with a snap so no other words could rush out.

But Cam just smiled. 'If I know my mother, it won't be a formal style of restaurant. Whatever we wear for wandering around on the beach will do.'

Lally appreciated the way he said 'we', as though both of them had been stressing over this topic. Cameron Travers truly was a kind and generous man, one whose smile disappeared when his mother's name was mentioned. That knowledge made Lally concerned, and a little sad, because she didn't think she was imagining this.

Cam said quietly, 'It will be nice to have company while I visit Mum.'

And just like that, he made Lally feel wanted, needed and let in; the idea of going away with him seemed totally appropriate despite anything she'd just been thinking, even while they were standing here in their bathing suits discussing it. Yes, they were covered in beach towels, too, but that was hardly the point.

Lally wasn't sure if she wanted to understand the point any more, to be honest. Because she had a suspicion it would end up being something to do with still being way too aware of her gorgeous boss, and now having far too many emotional connections towards him as well.

A genuine interest in him had developed—an appreciation for his cleverness and imagination, a need to look after him. Concern about his relationship with his mother.

But she didn't want to let him into her personal life. Not the history part of it, anyway. *Do you, Lally?*

Cameron touched her arm with his fingers, the lightest of touches. 'So, do we have a plan? Leave first thing tomorrow morning with a couple of days' clothes, some buckets and strong plastic bags for the pebbles?'

'Yes. We have a plan.' Lally's skin tingled where his fingers rested against her.

Well, tomorrow she would be stronger.

Tomorrow she would be totally strong.

'I'd best go see about what I need to pack.' She excused herself and went inside. She wasn't removing herself from the way of temptation—that wasn't necessary, because Lally Douglas had her world, her attitudes, her thoughts and her feelings completely under control.

Oh, yes, she did!

CHAPTER NINE

'I MEANT to check the forecast for the next two days for this area.' Cam made the statement as they climbed from his convertible onto an isolated stretch of beach. It was mid-afternoon.

After the long trip, it was good to step out into such beautiful surrounds. The beach was not ideal for swimming; the sea looked too rough for that, but there was sand, the smell of salt water, gorgeous sky and sea extending until they melded their shades of blue together on the horizon.

Lally seemed happy, anyway. She breathed in a deep breath as they got out of the car and her face had relaxed into an expression of pleasure.

Cam told himself not to dwell too much on that look, to think rather about the business end of this trip, such as making sure it would work for Lally. For that reason he couldn't quite keep the self-directed disapproval from his tone as he went on, 'I usually think of those sorts of things, but, even though I spent hours working on business and writing and that should have meant I was totally focused on all the different things on my agenda, I didn't consider the weather.'

He'd focused on his business matters, had prepared instructions to leave for the site boss in case he and Lally weren't back to speak to the guy by mid-afternoon Monday and had worked on his writing. He was well on track for his deadline now.

Perhaps Cam had overlooked the weather because he'd been trying to avoid some of his thoughts. Thoughts that had to do with whether it was wise to take Lally on this trip. He'd touched her arm after they'd been swimming last night, just touched her, and all of his senses had gone on alert again. Cam couldn't—one hundred percent could not—allow himself to be so overwhelmed by her. He had to resist desiring her.

Cam needed to focus on professionalism where Lally was concerned. Wanting to understand her, know all about her, know her secrets—he couldn't pursue that.

'The weather looks fine. I don't think we'll have any problems in that respect.' Lally spoke after casting a brief glance at the sky.

'Here's hoping you're right. But I'm leaving the top up on the car anyway. I don't trust coastal weather, it can change very quickly.' Cam took two buckets from the trunk, lined them with thick plastic bags and led the way onto the beach. If he treated this time as perfectly ordinary, that was what it would become eventually—wouldn't it?

And he might do better if he didn't touch her. At all. 'Let's see if we can find some nice, coloured pebbles and stones for your mosaic. I'm not sure if I'll be able to help or just be the "carry person" for you. I guess that'll depend on how specific you need your choices to be.'

'At first I'll only know what I want when I spot it, but, once I know, I don't see why you won't be able to find similar pebbles and stones and help gather them.'

Lally wanted to create the mosaic for Cam, and perhaps a little for herself. Maybe her relatives were right and it was past time for her to explore her artistic ability. She shouldn't feel that. She had no right to feel that.

She did feel happy and full of anticipation. About the work; it had nothing to do with the idea of strolling along beaches with a gorgeous man. A man who had the ability to turn her senses and her emotions to mush just by letting her see into the depths of his eyes.

Oh, Lally. That's not a helpful thought to have!

'You're quite sure you're happy with the style and design I want to use for the mosaic?' She'd been up later than she should have been last night working on the fine-tuning of that design. Cam had been restless too. Lally had heard that, but only because she'd been awake anyway. He always tried hard not to disturb her sleep.

With ideas buzzing in her mind, Lally had sketched out her plan for the mosaic and had noted what colours she'd use for the various parts of it. She'd shown those plans to Cam this morning before they'd left the apartment. She thought about them again now to try to help her control her wayward thoughts.

'I'm totally fine with it. You're the artist at work in this situation, Lally. What you say about it goes.'

Cam had been very supportive of her ideas earlier too.

Lally rubbed her hands together. 'Let's see if we can find some suitable pebbles.'

Lally strolled the first part of the beach. She looked at pebbles scattered here and there, bent to examine a shiny, flat rock weathered into smoothness by time and tide. Truly she didn't think once about how good Cam looked in his jeans-shorts that reached just below his knees, running shoes and T-shirt. Not once.

Lally wore white capri-pants, runners and a red, short-sleeved blouse. Lately she'd been reaching more often for the few brighter clothes she had in her wardrobe.

You've been reaching for bright clothes, like the dress Cam purchased for you that night.

Well, it wasn't as though she couldn't give herself permission to wear whatever colours she wanted to wear.

Really? You don't think that's just one indication that you're attracted to Cam and you want to attract his attention right back the same way you worked to attract Sam's attention six years ago?

What did one have to do with the other? Lally suppressed a frown.

'Is that stone a yes as a keeper, or a no?' Cam held the two empty pails in his hands. He gestured to the stone she was turning over and over in her hand.

'Oh, um…' Lally glanced at the stone blankly and back up into Cam's face. He hadn't shaved this morning, and her fingers itched to run through the light covering of beard growth. The texture would be prickly and silky at once.

If he kissed her, she would feel that silky prickliness against her mouth, brushing over the sensitive nerve-endings beneath her lower lip. It might not be smart, but Lally wanted Cam to give her that kiss. She glanced into his eyes and caught an equally aware, desire-filled expression there.

So why not just give in and kiss him, get a second taste of something that had felt rather like paradise?

How could one girl, who didn't even want to

be involved in such a way, miss a man's kiss after having it just once? How could she miss it enough to think such thoughts when they were dangerous to her emotional well-being? She searched Cam's eyes for the answer. But she wasn't sure if she wanted to find it.

Then she remembered a different question. 'The stone is smooth, beautifully rounded and a good colour. It's definitely a keeper.' She dropped it into the pail. She was supposed to be shopping for mosaic materials, not wishing she could kiss her boss.

Cam steered her in the direction of a ridge of pebbles that had been thrown up by the tide.

Lally bent to look and forced her mind to focus on the task of examining them and picking up the ones she thought had the best colours. She didn't want to think about any of the rest of it.

For the first while, Lally was uneasy as they gathered their pebbles. But Cam was a good help, standing patiently while she chose stones, picking out others that complemented the colours and shapes she'd chosen, and eventually she began to relax.

'Did you have any painting lessons at all? Non-traditional ones, I mean?' Cam asked as she sifted a handful of pebbles through her fingers.

'I painted a little during high school. Art classes, how to paint fruit in a bowl, that sort of thing. But I stopped after that.' Lally dropped a few pebbles into the bucket and bent to scoop up more.

Cam reached down at the same time and their fingers brushed. The sound of the sea ebbing and flowing on the shoreline seemed louder as Lally's breath stopped. Her gaze turned to Cam's face and got caught in the deep green of his eyes.

'Sorry. I wasn't looking.'

'I should let you check them first.'

They both went to get up, and Lally's sneaker sank into the damp sand. It made a squishing sound, and she couldn't hold back a slight smile. 'Do you know? I wish I could feel the sand beneath my toes. I haven't walked barefoot on a beach in ages.'

'So take your shoes off and get the full experience.' Cam said it in a teasing tone. His lips quirked and he bent to remove first one shoe, then the other.

His encouragement could have stabbed right through her. For wasn't that exactly what she'd done to get herself in trouble in the past—been a hedonist? Indulged in what she wanted while blindly ignoring all warning signs that she might be headed for trouble?

That wasn't the same, Lally. You're just walking on the beach. Lally removed her shoes.

They abandoned both pairs right there, just like that. Well, Cam seemed more than comfortable. And what was the harm, really?

'No one will take them.' Cam glanced about. 'It's totally deserted here.'

He was right about that. When he set the bucket down and held out his hand to her, a little thrill went through Lally before she placed her hand in his and let him lead her to the water's edge.

Cool sea-foam washed over her feet and splashed against her ankles. Cam's hand felt warm and firm in comparison with the skin of her palm. As the water rolled out again, the sand sucked away beneath Lally's feet.

'I do love that sensation.' She glanced up at

Cam and smiled. 'It's sort of icky and wonderfully good all at once.'

Cam laughed and his gaze softened as he looked into her eyes. There was such tenderness in that one glimpse of time. His hand tightened on hers; Lally realised they were still holding hands and told herself that should stop—but she didn't want to stop it. Particularly not when he looked at her this way.

Oh, but she needed to stop it, most of all because of that look; Lally broke away. 'We'd better get back to looking for pebbles. It's what we're here for—the mosaic. I want to do a good job of it for you.'

So they searched for pebbles and gathered quite a few. Lally loved the texture, the smoothness rounded into the stones by the constant movement, time smoothing off the edges. She glanced at Cam and thought, if only life could be that simple. Her six-year-old edges were still way too sharp.

Cam crouched down to sift through some pale-white stones. He played them through his fingers. From where she stood nearby, Lally had a view of the top of his head, the way his hair grew, the strength of the back and side of his neck and all of his face in profile.

'What do you think of these ones?' He looked up, caught her gaze on him and the green of his eyes darkened.

Lally's breath caught as her pulse sped up and her emotions responded to the expression in his eyes. He smiled then, and his smile was everything a woman could dream about. She wanted to melt into a puddle at his feet. She could have done that easily.

'The pebbles look good. Yes, I'd like to keep those ones, and I have some more.' Her fist closed about the ones she had gathered. She stepped forward and dropped them into the bucket beside him. 'I, um, I'll look further afield. Over there.' She gestured randomly and forced herself to strike out away from him.

He let her go. That was good because they couldn't be like this. *She* couldn't be like this. When had she become emotionally involved to the degree that she couldn't look at him in profile without wanting to step forward, wrap her arms around him, hold him and not let go?

'We'd better think about going if we're to meet my mother at the allotted time,' Cam said decisively as he stepped across the beach towards her about an hour later. He'd kept her supplied with buckets, but otherwise had left her alone.

Lally glanced up and her heart did it again—leapt, opened up, melted. She came forward with her current bucket brimming with stones; a mantra played in her head that she should play this cool, not let him see how he impacted on her.

'That was good timing. I think I have enough of any colours I can get from this beach.' She glanced down at her bucket and as she did failed to look where she was putting her foot. 'Ouch!'

A sharp sensation spread through her heel.

'Let me see.' Cam set his bucket down in the sand and had his fingers shackled firmly about her upper arm before she could even think.

It was natural to wrap her fingers around his strong forearm and use him for balance while she held her foot off the ground.

Cam looked at her foot, gently taking it in his other hand and turning it until he could see the bottom. Then he looked down into the sand.

'You've cut it on a rock. It doesn't look too deep, but it should be cleaned and dressed. Let's get you to the car so we can take care of it properly.'

'I might need your arm so I can hop along—' Lally got that much out before he swept her up into his arms and her thoughts fractured.

Consciousness of the sting in her foot faded as Cam's warm chest pressed against her arm and shoulder and his arms held her securely.

She'd been held by him like this before, at night at the top of the small, Adelaide-style skyscraper.

The whimsical thought brushed through her mind as her hands tightened together behind his neck. Lally told herself under no circumstances was she to stroke that neck, or in any other way reveal how being held by him made her feel.

You don't think that melting into him like a boneless blob might give him a hint?

'Okay. Let's sit you here and I'll take a proper look.' Cam eased her into the passenger seat of the convertible and seemed to release his hold on her reluctantly. He knelt at her feet and checked the wound. 'I've got a first aid kit. I think I can take care of this with cleaning solution and a couple of butterfly strips.'

'It probably only needs a plaster. Really, most of the sting has gone already.' Lally felt silly with her foot clasped in his hand and with him fussing over her. Silly and conscious of him all at once. 'It's just a cut. I'm sure if we clean it...' She leaned forward to try to take a look.

Cam tightened his fingers on her foot. '*I'll* clean it. You just sit tight and look beautiful.' He reached past her to open the glove compartment and pulled out the first-aid kit. He rummaged through it for the items he wanted. 'I've got a bandage too, so I can wrap that around it to make sure it all stays together when you put your shoe back on over the top.'

Lally sat back and let him take care of her, and he did, handling her foot gently and making sure he cleaned the wound thoroughly before he put on the steri-strips and covered it all in a bandage. He jogged back to the beach and retrieved both their pairs of shoes and the collection of stones, and helped her put her shoes on.

He was once again on his knees at her feet, a

strong man who seemed completely comfortable kneeling before her, looking after her.

When he glanced up and caught her studying him, his gaze darkened as it had back on the beach—except now there was nowhere for Lally to go, nothing to do but acknowledge the way he made her feel.

His hands bracketed the seat on either side of her legs as he leaned closer. 'I don't like that you got hurt.' His gaze was locked on her lips.

'It wasn't hurt badly, and you looked after me.' He'd told her to sit back and look beautiful. His eyes had taken in the wildness of her hair and Lally had *felt* beautiful, lovely, appealing and desirable. She realised she hadn't let herself feel that way for a long time.

His expression made her feel that way now. Lally caught her breath and a reserve inside her that had held together for six years frayed rather noticeably around its edges.

'Lally.' He murmured her name and leaned closer.

Lally heard her name and the warning in his tone as he spoke it.

Don't let me, his tone seemed to say.

But she was too busy reacting, and that reaction was to lean towards him while he leaned towards her until they were almost nose-to-nose. She could smell the blunted, woodsy scent of his aftershave lotion where it had blended with his skin.

He smelled good. Lally wanted to press her nose to his neck and just inhale him.

'God, Lally, when you look like that…' Cam broke off and closed the remaining distance between them.

CHAPTER TEN

CAM'S lips drew closer. Every pore of Lally's being wanted and needed his kiss. He kissed the side of her face in the shallow spot beneath her cheekbone. He kissed where her cheek creased when she smiled.

He kissed the edge of her lips with a teasing press; Lally turned her head and blindly sought the second full press of his lips to hers. She got it, and her eyelids felt way too heavy to hold open, so she let them flutter closed as he pressed more soft kisses to her lips, and she kissed him back just as softly.

The ocean rolled against the beach down on the shore. A seagull cried; Lally breathed Cam deep into her lungs and held him there.

His hands came up to clasp her shoulders, to brush gently over them and rub against her back.

His fingertips worshipped the softness of her skin, and he made a sighing sound as though he'd found exactly what he'd been looking for and just wanted to enjoy it.

That slow, detailed attention swept Lally away more effectively than anything else would have. It was as though Cam took time in his hands and stilled it so they could have this, indulge in it and experience it in its fullest measure.

His lips pressed to hers.

Her mouth opened to him because he made what they were sharing feel so completely safe, so utterly right.

Lally forced her eyes open to seek his; slumberous green looked at her. He seemed so at ease, restful to the point almost of being sleepy. Lally didn't know why that response in him made her feel powerful, but it did.

'Lally.' His fingers sifted through her hair, caught the long strands and played with them, before he pressed those fingers with just the right amount of pressure against the base of her skull and drew her forward so he could deepen their kiss.

Their tongues met, stroked.

Lally didn't know how he did it, but somehow in his gentleness and focus Cam encouraged her to take whatever she wanted of him. He offered his tongue. She drew it into her mouth and explored the taste and texture. She felt her back arch as he gave a soft sound of pleasure and his arms drew her closer still.

His fingers pressed against her shoulders until their bodies were chest to chest. It felt good, it felt right, and Lally relaxed even more.

She didn't know when the kiss changed, when slow became deep, when sultry became focused, when restful became hungry and desperate became need-filled; it just happened. Cam was kissing her utterly then, his mouth locked over hers. All of his focus and all of hers was fixed on this exchange, these sensations.

Even as her hands rose to his chest, to his shoulders, Lally knew this kiss was different. This kiss was not Sam kissing her, relying on his charm to lead her to do whatever he wanted, to overwhelm her so she didn't think about his motives, so she didn't suspect them.

This kiss wasn't like Cam's last kiss either. That had been wonderful. This was more, so much more that Lally could not remember why she shouldn't do this. She needed this, *had* to do this. Lally *liked* Cam, admired him, was attracted to him not only physically but to his thought processes, his creativity, his business acumen, drive, ambition, attention to detail, enthusiasm for his work, imagination…

How could she fight this kind of attraction? It was more than she had ever felt for any other man, Sam included.

That fact got through to Lally as nothing else had. If she let herself follow this path, where would it end? How capable would she be of getting hurt? How could anything be *more* than Sam had been in her life? Sam had irrevocably changed it.

Lally had to stop this. Even now her instincts fought her mind. Her lips remained right where they were, pressed to Cam's. Her hands slid to Cam's upper arms, a precursor to letting go, but her fingers clasped those arms. Lally dropped her hands but they slid away from him slowly.

It was Cam who broke the kiss itself, his gaze already searching hers. What Lally imagined he saw there was echoed in his own expression.

Desire and caution, want and the need to stop.

'Lally, we have to—'

'We have to stop—' Lally lost the words in the depths of his eyes, found them again in the drive inside her that insisted she keep herself safe, that she not get hurt again, not yield to feelings for a man who wouldn't value them, not make a mess, create guilt—oh, so many things.

Cam was her boss, he was wealthy, famous and amazing, and Lally was the temporary housekeeper and assistant. Cam was very much out of her league. In the end he was as much out of her reach, as Sam *should* have been, if for other reasons. And Sam was part of Lally's reason now, that tainted history.

The resignation in Cam's eyes told her he felt the same way about this, at least to the extent that he knew this had to stop, that it wouldn't be wise for them. What were his reasons?

'We should get going. Your foot's okay? It's

not hurting you?' Cam put his shoes on while she settled herself properly in her seat.

'It's fine now that it's cleaned and wrapped. And we don't want to be late for dinner with your mother.' Lally spoke the words through kiss-swollen lips, over the taste of him that was still on her tongue, trying to make sense when she couldn't think straight.

Cam searched her eyes for a moment before he closed her car door, crossed in front and got into the driver's seat. Just a few moments with those broad shoulders in motion, his long legs eating up the ground until he slid behind the wheel, and Lally couldn't concentrate again.

'Would you like the top down again?' Cam glanced her way.

Lally quickly nodded. 'The breeze is nice.'

She didn't care about her hair getting whipped about; that could be fixed when they arrived. Maybe the wind would blow this lapse of control away.

Cam got things organised. Then he sat there with the engine idling and finally turned his gaze her way. 'Lally…'

'Don't.' She shook her head. 'Please. We have to see your mother. Can we just…do that?'

So they went.

'Here we are.' Cam drew the car to a halt in a restaurant's small parking-lot. 'Hopefully Mum will be here and won't have changed her plans without letting me know.'

'Does she do that often?' Lally asked as they made the short walk to the restaurant's entrance.

'It happens.' Cam's mother did a lot of things he didn't always like. 'How's the foot? If it's hurting, I can help you.'

'Oh, no, it's okay—and I wouldn't want your mother to think—' Lally broke off.

But not before Cam saw the memory of their kisses cross her face. Lally might have set out to say she didn't want his mother to think she was anything other than able to look after herself, or something like that, but her words had quickly led her thoughts elsewhere.

Cam could identify with that, because all his thoughts seemed to lead elsewhere at the moment.

And all those 'elsewhere' roads led to one

place: the kissing Lally place. His lack of control around her was substantial, it seemed. Cam wasn't exactly proud of that and yet he couldn't regret what they'd shared.

'Then I guess I won't carry you inside.' He said it with a smile that took effort at first. But he thought his mother might actually do a double take if she saw him walk into the restaurant carrying Lally clutched to his chest like a prize, and his smile became more natural.

He turned to her as they made their way inside. 'There's about an eighty-percent chance we'll be meeting someone else as well as my mother for dinner.'

'I'm not sure what you mean.' Lally seemed to be just on the edge of nervous.

Or maybe that was left over from what had passed between them back at the beach. Cam glanced at her. Even hobbling a little, she still managed to look graceful. He looked again. He realised his mother might be likely to bring 'a friend' yet again to meet him, but Cam wanted to show Lally off to his mother. That was very much a first.

As your employee. You want to show her off as your employee.

Yeah.

Right. That was what he wanted. That was no doubt what had driven him to kiss her again back there at the beach, lose complete sight of where they were. It was what he'd told himself he would and wouldn't do when it came to Lally.

Cam wasn't sure he wanted to think about his motives for that. Somehow they appeared to be linked to something far too deep inside him that he'd thought he had worked out. He *did* have it all worked out!

'I guess you'd say Mum's a free spirit. She's not someone who will pin down to anything for long, but when it comes to relationships that's not a lesson she's been able to acknowledge within herself. She keeps leaping in and backing out again just as quickly.'

'Oh.' Lally gave a calm nod. 'I have an older cousin who's like that—revolving-door relationships. I don't know how she deals with the stress, although, now that I think about it, she manages to walk away apparently unscathed each time. I couldn't do it.' She fell abruptly silent.

Cam had a feeling it had occurred to both of them at once that they weren't really in the best position to discuss this as uninvolved observers. 'We can't be—'

'Well, there you are. Cameron, come and meet Tom; he's such a darling. I don't know where I'd be without him.' His mother stepped forward as she spoke the flow of words, hugged him quickly and stepped back.

The obligatory hug was over for another year, and it had happened so quickly that Cam had almost missed it.

Men weren't supposed to feel the lack of that kind of thing, were they? Yet it occurred to Cam in this moment that he'd missed a lot of real, genuine hugs in his lifetime. Lally would never hug half-heartedly like that. Cam just knew this.

He'd felt it for himself when she'd held him, and everything inside him had relaxed and felt as though it could rest and be still.

That stillness wasn't something Cam under-stood, and he hadn't truly thought about it in relation to Lally until now. But she gave him that feeling. It was as though somehow being around her helped him to find peace or something.

And what are you now, Travers? Some kind of tortured soul? For crying out loud!

Cam turned his gaze to his mother. 'Hello, Mum. This is Lally. Lally, meet my mother, Dana.' He shook hands with—*John? No, that was the last one.* 'Hello, Tom.'

'What have you been doing, Cameron? Dull old business things, I suppose, with a bit of writing thrown in on the side?' His mother picked up her menu and started to scan it. 'You should rest more. Weariness isn't attractive, you know.'

'Insomnia isn't quite the same as weariness, Mum. And I always do try to rest.' Cam said it gently; he didn't expect Dana to really listen. He drew a breath to turn the conversation elsewhere.

'I think Cam deals really well with his insomnia.' Lally's words came softly into the conversation. 'It can't be easy to have all those long hours to get through, knowing you can't rest as much as you'd like to be able to.'

Cam hadn't expected her to speak. The

support behind the words touched him. He stared into liquid brown eyes and felt much of the tension over seeing his mother again ease out of him.

With a few soft words, Lally had him in a better place with things. Cam needed to make sure his housekeeper and assistant was in a good place too, because beneath the surface of her cheerful attitude he could see a hint of unhappiness that he suspected might have been for his sake. His mother had turned her head to speak quietly to Tom for a moment.

Cam touched Lally's hand beneath the table. 'Thank you,' he murmured so only she could hear him. 'Mum doesn't mean any harm. We're not very close, you know? But I still like to see her occasionally. She's the only relative I've got.'

Could those words reassure a woman whose life to a large degree seemed to revolve around her love for her big extended family? It wasn't a topic Cam could cover further now, at any rate.

'You should just take sleeping pills, Cameron.' His mother tossed these words out. They were an easy solution, a fast solution;

Dana was good at offering those and then forgetting all about whatever issue had arisen in the first place.

She just wasn't good at seeing that some things didn't *have* fast, easy solutions. 'I'm sure after a few days of those your body would retrain and you'd be fine.'

'Lally's trying some bush-food remedies to see if they'll help,' Cam offered with a determined smile. 'And I have felt more relaxed in the past while.' That was down to Lally herself, in Cam's opinion, but he kept that thought to himself.

And now he really wanted to change the topic.

'I see.' His mother looked back at her menu then glanced at her watch. 'We should make our selections. I'm sure the waiter will be along at any moment.'

Lally blinked just once before she lowered her gaze to her menu.

Cam had the odd urge to take her hand again beneath the table and this time keep it in his clasp.

Instead, he turned his attention to choosing a meal.

Tom spoke, bringing up an interest in fishing and four-wheel-driving. 'What do you drive, Cameron?'

Cam gave the older man the make and model of his convertible. 'I like—'

'The fresh air.' Lally glanced at him and smiled. 'It was nice this morning, wasn't it? Coastal roads, warm weather and a sea breeze.'

'What exactly is your relationship to Cameron, Lally?' his mother suddenly asked nosily.

Cam opened his mouth to answer, somewhat protectively. His mum's tendency to stomp all over people's privacy with her questions was something Cam hadn't taken into account when he'd invited Lally along for this. He should have thought about it.

But Lally beat him to it. 'I'm working as a temporary housekeeper to Cam while he's in Adelaide.' She smiled. 'And building him a pebble mosaic for the courtyard of his property development there, while he creates his latest crime story to keep readers on the edges of their seats.'

'Oh.' Mum seemed to be somewhat at a loss.

'So, you're a bit of a Jill of all trades? Stone masonry is an unusual career choice for a woman.'

'Well, pebble mosaics are a little different to stone masonry.' Lally quickly outlined her vision for the mosaic. 'I'm looking forward to doing the work, anyway.'

'And I'm looking forward to seeing the end result.' Cam closed his menu. Because he didn't want his mum cross-questioning Lally for the rest of the meal, he really did change the subject now. 'Catch of the day for me. You can't beat fresh fish, isn't that right, Tom?'

They discussed fishing and real estate through the main course. When he'd first got enough money to do it, Cam had bought his mother a home in Sydney and had invited her to settle there. He'd hoped to have her nearer, to be able to see her more.

That had been a vain hope. His mother had taken the property, immediately rented it out, and gone on her way travelling, content so long as no one asked her to put down roots.

'Remember, the house is always there for you, Mum.' He didn't know what made him say it.

Dana gave him an uncomprehending look. 'Well, and so it should be. It was a pay-off for the years I sacrificed to raise you. I deserve that rental income to allow me to travel in my motor home wherever I want to go.'

'You could change for the right man—settle down in a real home,' Tom muttered beneath his breath. He followed it up with a teasing smile, but he frowned and pushed his dinner plate away at the same time.

Cam glanced at his watch. Only a little over half an hour had passed since they'd sat down; it felt like much longer.

'I have family in Queensland and the Torres Strait islands,' Lally said as she pushed a fat, golden chip around her plate with her fork. 'My mother tries to get up that way every couple of years. I've enjoyed making the trips with her a few times.'

Lally glanced briefly towards him.

Ah, Lally. Don't care about this. It just isn't worth it.

The conversation segued to a discussion of bush foods and other cuisine. That took them through the rest of the meal. When it ended and Cam's mother mentioned coffee, Cam shook his head and stood.

'We need to push on, find a suitable place to stay this evening. It was…good to see you.' He nodded to Tom. He didn't bother trying to kiss Dana's cheek or hug her. She hadn't got up and clearly didn't intend to.

Instead, Cam took Lally's arm in a gentle clasp, nodded to his mum and Tom once again and led Lally out of the restaurant.

'Your mother seems very…autonomous,' Lally said as diplomatically as she could.

Cam saw her effort to avoid saying so much else, and he appreciated it for what it was. He shook off his mood because there was no point and he didn't want to spoil the rest of their evening. 'She always has been. I try.'

Cam *did* try. He kept a one-way stream of communication with Dana throughout the year, using whatever medium of contact she made available to him. The contact just didn't come back his way very often.

'Did your mother look into your insomnia

when you were younger?' Lally asked with a frown.

'She didn't acknowledge it as anything more than a child being annoying about not wanting to sleep.' There'd been a lot of nights spent lying awake. The settings had changed all the time, but the end results had been the same.

Lally seemed to fight with herself for a moment before the need for expression finally got the better of her. 'Your insomnia probably started as a result of you being picked up and moved around all the time. If you'd received the right kind of attention back then…'

'That's a long way back. I don't think it was that.' Yet Cam had developed that problem as a child. He'd just assumed he got it from the gene pool of whoever had fathered him, that it was a genetic issue, not one that might have developed from his circumstances. 'I've lived away from that environment for a long time now.'

'And kept moving around, the way your mother always has.' Lally searched his eyes. 'I'm not saying you shouldn't travel if that's what keeps you happy, but maybe you haven't had a decent chance at finding that kind of peace to allow you to properly rest?'

Cam opened his mouth to say that moving around was as necessary to him as it was to his mother. Then he closed it again, because he wasn't quite sure if it *was* as necessary as he had always thought.

Yet, if it wasn't, why did he keep on the move all the time, constantly searching, looking for the next challenge, the next brick in the road, the next great book idea and property-development idea? 'I guess travelling has been a way to fill all the time that yawns in front of me.'

Cam just didn't know what else it meant. And he felt oddly uncertain about the whole topic. 'Let's go find a nice bed and breakfast for the night.'

'Yes. Let's.' Lally didn't push the topic. Instead, she drew a deep breath and smiled as they reached his car and climbed in.

They got on the road, and Cam slowly forgot about the visit with his mother.

Instead he took the opportunity to gently grill Lally about her family situation. Lally seemed to need them so much, and Cam wanted to try to understand where she stood in relation to all that.

He wanted to understand the why of her needs, and whether that somehow related to the occasional sadness he saw in her eyes.

'I'm looking forward to getting back to my usual work among the family after this assignment is over.' Lally glanced his way. 'I'm happy with you as well. I just need to do that for my family. It's safe—' Lally cut the words off and frowned.

They passed through one small place, but the accommodation didn't look particularly inviting. Cam chose to move on. He'd researched a bed and breakfast on-line in the next town that had looked good in the photos.

Lally leaned her head back against the seat and became silent. A few minutes later, she fell asleep.

CHAPTER ELEVEN

CAM reached into the car, lifted his slumbering housekeeper into his arms, carried her inside the bed and breakfast, up the staircase and into the only room they had free.

The rain had just stopped. It had pelted down for the last hour as he made the slow trip here. Cam had sat the last few minutes out in the parked car, right outside the B&B, with Lally gently sleeping in the seat beside him. She slept so peacefully—Cam could envy that!

She must have been exhausted, and Cam felt at least partly to blame for that. He'd been disturbing her sleep since she'd first moved in with him. He knew it, even though he'd tried to be quiet at night when he moved around in their apartment.

He should put her out into one of the other apartments. How long would it take to gather up enough furniture to make her comfortable? He could order the lot over the phone in about twenty minutes.

Cam's arms tightened about his burden that felt like no burden at all. He'd be quieter, make sure he didn't disturb her in future. He didn't want to move her out.

'Are we there already?' Lally murmured in a sleepy voice and then seemed to realise she wasn't on her feet. Confusion filled her gaze and she blinked at him with wide eyes that quickly changed from slumberous to conscious and softened as they locked on his face.

One look from her, one glimpse into those un-guarded eyes, and all Cam wanted...

Well, he couldn't have what he wanted. If he'd let himself wonder otherwise, spending time with his mother today had concreted the fact that he just couldn't go there with Lally.

She deserved more than someone who'd pack up and move around all the time, who would not want to settle down somewhere with her, not want babies and a picket fence. Not know how to give that even if he had wanted it.

You could have babies and a courtyard and a big, old family home that you're converting into apartments right now. You already know it would work quite well as a home.

Since when had Cam started to think about that big, old place as a potential home, rather than a sound business-investment? Let alone think about settling down. It was out of the question; totally and utterly out of the question for him.

Cam set Lally down in the small living area of the room and backed away. 'Eh, you fell asleep in the car. There's been a storm, so I drove us to this B&B. All they had was this room, and they told me all the other accommodation in the area is booked out. The bad weather took a few travellers by surprise, apparently.'

He rammed his hand through his hair upwards from the base at the back. 'So, eh, I can sleep in the car.'

'Oh.' Lally blinked, blinked again and glanced around them, taking in the surroundings, the double bed beside the bank of windows. 'Well, um…'

'Yeah. I'll go get our things. At least I can have a hot shower.' Cam swung about and left the room.

As Cam left, Lally drew a deep breath and tried to calm herself. She wasn't nervous, though maybe that feeling would catch up in a minute. She was just trying to come to terms with waking up in his arms like that. Had she melted into him before she woke up? What if she'd talked in her sleep? Snored? Kissed him? Dribbled?

Oh, for heaven's sake; she was just snoozing.

Snoozing right through a fierce storm, apparently. And Cam had sat with her in the car then carried her inside. He must have a lot of patience.

Well, the man couldn't sleep himself. He was probably used to needing a lot of patience to get through all those hours when he wanted to be asleep but wasn't. Maybe he'd got some vicarious satisfaction out of knowing she was sleeping.

And maybe Lally was letting her imagination run away with her so she wouldn't have to think about sharing a room with her boss tonight.

'Room service,' Cam quipped as he stepped into the room and dumped their bags. He glanced at her face, and shoved his hands in his pockets. 'I said it already, Lally—I'll sleep in the car.'

'Yes, well, you see, that's the problem—I can't let you do that. You'd be so uncomfortable. It's a great car, but it's not made for sleeping in.' She couldn't let him do that. 'There's really nowhere else we could go for the night?'

He was shaking his head before she even finished speaking. 'There's nowhere nearby, and they seem to think there'll be a second storm-front.'

'I don't know why I did that. Slept, I mean. It must have been all the fresh air and wandering on the beach earlier.'

'Fresh air and exercise has that effect on a lot of people.' He set their bags against the wall out of the way. 'They're offering winter warmers in the dining room: would you like to come down, have a hot drink, at least?'

Lally nodded. 'That would be nice. I'd better tidy up.'

At least they had their own bathroom tucked behind a door. Lally picked up her handbag that Cam had kindly brought in for her, stepped into the bathroom, shut the door and splashed water over her face. Her hair was springy from the weather. She knew better than to brush it. If she did, it would just get springier.

So she twisted and tied it in a loose knot to keep it half under control, applied some lipstick and a spritz of perfume and called the job done. 'I'm ready.'

'You look lovely,' Cam murmured, then took her arm and led her from the room. 'Let's go see what's on offer.'

Lally hadn't been alert enough to think about the intimacy of the room. Now she tried to absorb his compliment and felt a glow come over her, because being told by a man that she looked great would naturally give her a glow, wouldn't it?

It was nothing to do with this specific man. Any man saying that would have had the same impact.

Oh, she really wished her thoughts wouldn't step in and question her like that. Sometimes ignorance, or at the very least letting herself think whatever suited best, truly could be bliss. It was better than delving too deeply into the truth.

Like the truth of knowing you need to share a room with him tonight?

Maybe she should offer to sleep in the car.

But he wouldn't allow it, and Lally knew that.

'It looks like that table is free.' Cam led the way to a small table in the corner and they took their seats. The table was beside a window and outside streaks of drizzling rain ran down the pane of glass.

'I'd thought we might have to sit at one large, long table and share our company with everyone else,' Lally observed.

Since when did you become a hermit, Lally Douglas? Usually you love big dinners with lots of people around.

That was when she was with her family. This was different. She didn't want to admit that she wanted Cam all to herself.

She must be still sleepy, not thinking straight. 'Not that I'd have minded,' Lally declared a little too loudly and with a little too much emphasis, and felt telling heat creep into her face. 'I'd have been quite happy to share. I'd have been quite happy to share news with the other guests, have a bit of a chat. Well, the table setting is nice, don't you think?'

Lally gestured at it and told herself the fat red candle in its old-fashioned brass holder didn't look at all romantic, nor did her boss look equally so with candlelight playing across the angles and shadows of his face.

He was grinning, just the slightest bit—as one was wont to do when a woman blabbered, Lally pointed out to herself with an inner frown.

The guesthouse manager came to their table and gave a friendly nod. 'We're not overly fancy here, but we've got a really nice soup on offer, cake or dessert, plus tea, coffee and hot chocolate.' He rattled off a description of each choice.

Lally was surprised to discover she actually felt a little hungry. 'I'd love to try the soup.'

They both opted for that to start off.

Lingering over the supper would use up some of the time until they could go to bed and hope to sleep.

Well, Lally would hope to sleep. Cam didn't at the best of times; she doubted he'd do better when he didn't even have the bed to himself.

Thinking about getting into bed with him was really not a good idea when she was sitting across a romantic table-setting from him.

'It's *not* a romantic table-setting,' she muttered, and fell silent.

'Water?' Cam judiciously ignored her comment and poured water for both of them from a carafe on the table. He passed her drink to her before taking a sip of his own.

Lally watched him drink and thought he even did that appealingly.

Do not let your thoughts start wandering where he's concerned. He's your boss. The boss and the housekeeper—got that? Good!

Maybe they could put a line of pillows down the middle of the bed or something. Or one of them could sleep rolled into a blanket so there was no chance that their bodies would touch. What did they call that in the old days—buffering? Bundling?

The soup arrived and Lally stirred her spoon through it. 'Mmm, I think it has some mushroom in it, beef and tomato, and I suspect some brown lentils. Basil, carrot; definitely parsnip. I'm not sure what else.'

Very good, Lally. Perhaps you could rabbit on about the soup some more, totally bore him under the table in the first five minutes.

'And some pasta whirls and green peas.' Cam dug his spoon around in his soup and glanced up at her through his lashes. 'There's also either sweet-potato or pumpkin. There's a reason they call some soups a meal in a bowl.'

In this case they were small, shallow bowls. Lally took the first mouth-watering sip of the soup and her respect for this tucked-out-of-the-way B&B rose even more. 'I wish I knew how they made this.'

'Would you like me to try to get the recipe for you?'

Lally wouldn't be surprised if he managed to charm the recipe out of the manager's chef or wife, or whoever did the cooking. 'Well, only if the opportunity comes up. My sister Tammy would love to cook this.'

They fell silent for a few minutes, simply enjoying the warming fare.

Lally thought about something else that was on her mind and said, 'I'm trying to imagine what it would be like to only have one relative and not see her very often.'

The manager removed the empty soup bowls and offered them a selection of desserts off a trolley. After they'd chosen, he left again with a murmur. Outside, the rain started to come down in thick sheets. It spattered against the window and made Lally glad to be inside. The memory of Cam's kiss earlier today rose in her mind, and she tried very hard to push it back out again. She was too vulnerable right now to let herself remember.

Cam glanced at the window and returned his gaze to her. The green of his eyes seemed particularly deep in the candlelight as he met her gaze. 'I see my mother when she's prepared to fit me into her schedule. Usually that's a couple of times a year. To be honest, though, I do try to keep a flow of text messages and things going her way; that amount of contact is enough for me.'

Because his mother didn't take much notice of him when they *did* meet. She didn't listen to the things he told her; she was a lot more interested in herself than she was in him. Lally suspected that Dana Travers might not bother even to respond to many of her son's communications at all.

The woman had acted as though having a home given to her as a reward for putting up with him as a child was more than her due. 'Was your mother always…?'

'Like what you saw today?' He shrugged his shoulders. 'I came up knowing she hadn't really wanted the responsibility of a child, but she did keep me with her. She just did it her way, I guess.'

'By travelling all the time.' Lally's eyebrows drew together. She was trying hard not to judge the other woman too harshly but it wasn't easy. 'You must have been very good academically to survive that kind of existence and still do well.'

'Books helped.' Cam took a spoonful of fluffy lemon mousse, let it slide over his tongue and swallowed it. 'Every town we went to, I read as many library books as I could before we moved on again. I guess that helped a lot with keeping me where I needed to be with schoolwork. That and a few understanding teachers here and there along the way. I spent a lot of time by myself while Mum…'

'Wasn't there?'

'Yeah. We lived and travelled in a camper van. I thought being left by myself was what happened to every kid.' He said it in a matter-of-fact tone, yet Lally felt certain he rarely if ever talked about this.

This amazing man had been more ignored into adulthood than raised. His mother had let him know he was an inconvenience to her. That was unkind, cruel, to a little boy. What had Dana been thinking?

She'd been thinking of herself, and not the impact that her attitude would have on her son.

And who are you to judge, Lally? You sent not one but three young boys away from their mother!

'You must have had a lot of nights when you went to sleep wondering where you'd be the next day.' Lally swallowed back her guilt.

'I did, but on the upside I got to see a lot of gum trees, caravan parks and bush campsites,' Cam quipped, and then fell silent. His eyebrows drew down and a thoughtful expression crossed his face before he sighed and shook his head. 'How's your dessert?'

'It's nice. I'm glad I chose the mousse too.' She dug her spoon into the dish and gave thanks that he hadn't discerned the tone of her thoughts. 'This tastes so good, I'm guessing there's got to be a gazillion calories in it. And that's just the portion I have on my spoon.'

Cam laughed, as she had hoped he would. They fell silent, finished their desserts, lingered over coffee and ended up talking about football teams, current affairs and whether it made sense to invest in gold bullion in today's economy.

It was relaxing and interesting. Relieved, Lally found herself looking into his eyes for the sheer pleasure of seeing the almost sleepy expression there.

But it was the slumberous look of a big, contented cat. There was leashed power behind it, an interest in her that was also leashed. Lally knew that, and sensual awareness built gently between them as they shared that exchange of glances, long, silent looks and casual conversation that was a cover for all that wasn't being said.

The dining room began to empty out, and

Cam gestured to her cup. 'Would you like me to try to rustle up another drink for you?'

'I've had enough, I think. I hope that I'll get at least *some* sleep tonight.' She stopped and bit her lip, because even mentioning that made this intimacy feel even more intimate.

'We'll go up.' Did his voice hold the slightest hint of inevitability?

Or was that all inside her?

He rose from the table and took her arm to guide her out of the room.

They trod the staircase in silence. As they moved upstairs, the sound of the rain became louder. It sounded so lovely, the water hitting the corrugated-iron roof of the old building, sluicing into the gutters and running down the drainpipes.

'I'll enjoy listening to that tonight for however long it lasts,' Cam commented as he unlocked the door to their room.

Their room. For the whole night. With Cam awake while she slept. 'I, um, I hope I don't snore or talk in my sleep.' Or cuddle up to him without realising it...

'I think any of that will be the least of our

worries,' Cam murmured. He closed his eyes for a moment and opened them with a question on his lips. 'Would you like to use the bathroom first, Lally, or will I go?'

He asked it so gently.

'I'll go first, if you don't mind.' She got her things, slipped into the bathroom and used the time under the shower to try to pull herself together.

When she came out in her nightwear—boy's shorts and a matching camisole top covered with the longer shirt she'd had on today—Cam glanced at her.

His gaze dropped to her bare legs for a split second and slid away again, and he scooped up his things and closed himself in the bathroom.

That hadn't been too bad. Really, she'd been worrying about nothing. Lally shrugged out of the shirt, lifted the covers of the bed on the side closest to the window and scooched under.

Cam stayed in the shower until he couldn't put off getting out any longer. He dried off, used his deodorant, tried not to think about the scent of Lally in the bathroom that had been tantalising him since he stepped in here and pulled on his boxers.

Though he considered getting back into his T-shirt, he pushed the thought away. Sleep was difficult enough, and he never slept in a shirt. Lally would already be in bed anyway, probably with the light out if his guess was on the mark. So it wasn't as though she'd be looking at him, and she'd seen him dressed in as little when they'd been in the swimming pool anyway.

Cam pushed the bathroom door open, oriented himself, clicked the light off and made his way to the bed.

The room was quite dark; that was probably a good thing. Cam lifted the covers, got into the bed, drew a slow, single breath and held it.

He could smell the sweet scent of Lally's deodorant, and the body gel she'd used in the shower. He could smell her, warm and soft and very, very close to him. Close enough that he could feel her body heat beside him in the bed.

'Goodnight, Cam. I hope you sleep at least a

little. I don't want my presence to add to your trouble with that.'

She sounded concerned, and a little breathless.

Cam wanted to pull her into his arms and kiss her until she was breathless for other reasons.

Yeah, that would work well. He'd get her in his arms, not want to let her go and it would go way beyond kissing.

Don't think about kissing her. Think of standing outside in that driving rain getting soaked and cold.

'Goodnight, Lally.' He doubted he would sleep a wink, but there was no need to tell her that. 'The main thing is for you to relax and sleep as much as you can. I'll be happy lying here listening to the rain. I can spend some time plotting the next part of my story in my head. I might write a scene where they stay in a B&B during a wild storm.'

'Story writing must be great that way.' She said it sleepily. 'You can utilise all your experiences.'

'I guess so, though I'm not about to claim that I've experienced any of the gory stuff I write in my books.' He accompanied his soft chuckle with a nod, and realised he could see the outline of her face and the soft glow of her eyes.

His vision had adjusted to the dark. The crack of light coming in beneath the door from the hallway was enough to allow him that much. That meant Lally had been able to see him from the moment he'd stepped out of the bathroom because she'd already been lying there, warm and soft.

Enough thinking about that!

'More pebble-collecting tomorrow? We've done well so far, don't you think?' It was an odd version of pillow talk, but it was better than wrapping his arms around her and kissing her until he went mad with need.

Need? Or desire, want? Well, of course it could only be desire and want. He wasn't capable of anything else.

'We have done well with the pebble collecting. I hope the rain stops before we get up tomorrow, otherwise we might not get anywhere with the rest of our search.' She yawned into her hand and tucked the covers more snugly about her chin. Beneath the blankets, her knee brushed against his leg as she shifted position.

'Oh, sorry.' She whipped her leg away and said breathlessly, 'It's not a very big bed for a double.'

'Standard size, I think.' But he knew what she meant. All he'd need to do was reach for her, tangle his legs with hers…

'Goodnight.' He uttered that single word and rolled over so he was facing away from her. Amazing just how much a man could want to resist making that one, small move.

Cam lay in the darkness and kept his breathing deep and even. Lally first lay very still and barely breathed at all, then wriggled this way and that before finally relaxing until her breathing evened out to something close to the pace and cadence of his.

She was asleep about two minutes later, fully immersed in it within half an hour.

The rain continued to fall outside the window. Cam rolled over again and gave himself a moment of looking at her face in repose in the dimness. He drew a deep breath and yawned.

His body did a weird thing; it sort of relaxed, even though he was still utterly aware of her. Well, he was a man, they were in bed, she was beautiful, he liked her and he already knew what she tasted like.

Cam sent his thoughts outside into the driving rain again to get them off that particular trail. Obviously he wasn't going to be totally relaxed in these circumstances, but even so he felt calm. Content. He felt like he did when he finally got exhausted enough to sleep, but also different. He wasn't about to pass out but he felt like he could drift away on a cloud or something.

Maybe he would think about his story a bit later. He yawned again and all his muscles relaxed.

For now, he really was tempted to just close his eyes for a bit.

He did that…and slept.

CHAPTER TWELVE

LALLY woke to the sound of a cloudburst. In the moment that she opened her eyes, she realised it was pre-dawn—dim but not entirely dark; maybe about four in the morning.

Then Lally became aware of so much else: the press of a man's warm body against her soft curves. Cam. The scent of him mixed with her scent in the warmth of the bed they shared. A heartbeat registered through the tips of her fingers where they lay against his bare chest. Strong arms wrapped around her, skin on skin where the camisole top left so much of her back, arms and chest bare.

And a chin tucked over the top of her head so that she was cuddled into him, as though he'd reached for her, put her there and hadn't wanted to let go.

Lally's breath caught and her senses exploded with a surge of desire and need while her emotions clamoured with the torn feelings that came from being in his arms. So many conflicted feelings; she hadn't anticipated any of them, yet they washed all through her.

Lally tried to blame her rioting feelings on suddenly finding herself in this position. What if she'd ended up here because *she* had rolled into his arms, cuddled up to him quite shamelessly? What if she'd done that while he was wide awake and he'd put up with it rather than waking her? She wouldn't have said Sam's name in her sleep, would she?

But Lally knew she would not have done that, because it wasn't Sam who'd filled her thoughts since the day she'd met Cameron. Sam hadn't filled her thoughts for a long time, other than with guilt.

Cam made a contented, sensual sound in his sleep and his arms tightened their hold about her. Lally's worries gave way to more immediate responses, and not all of those responses came out of the fact of their physical closeness.

That set it all off. She wanted his kisses and to be loved by him; she wanted his body—but she also wanted him to want her soul. Lally wanted Cameron far too much to be safe in that wanting.

'Easy, Lally.' Cam stroked the backs of his knuckles gently over her back. His words were slurred and relaxed, more asleep than awake. 'It's just rain. We're safe. We know where we are.'

The mumbled words said so much about Cam's attitude to feeling misplaced.

'I wasn't…' *Worried about that.* She heaved in a breath. Given that brought them even more chest-to-chest, that didn't exactly help. His voice had been all raspy, as though he'd been in a deep, deep sleep. 'I know we're safe. We're at the B&B after our pebble collecting and dinner with your mother.'

She threw that in just in case he needed to be reminded, so he could completely orient himself.

Lally cleared her throat and whispered into the night, 'Did you sleep like that for long?'

There was a beat of silence and then a slow, surprised, 'Out like a light, and I must have slept for about six hours. I fell asleep listening to you sleeping. I'd still have been asleep if you hadn't started to wake.' His voice deepened again. 'Not that I minded.'

There was a great deal of 'not minding' along with the surprise that he'd slept so well in those few words, maybe more than he'd meant to let slip.

Lally felt thrilled because she'd helped him sleep. How silly was that? He'd probably slept due to some totally different reason. Maybe rain falling helped him to sleep. Didn't people listen to recordings of water falling and things like that, for that reason?

But he'd have tried that and be doing it all the time, if it worked for him. Cam's hand curved against her shoulder. He barely moved it, and yet all of Lally's body responded with a deep and demanding command to arch into his touch.

Was it the early hour of the morning and the dimmed intimacy of the room that made his words sound like the most sensual thing she had heard? His touch an invitation, a hope and a promise?

Lally tried desperately to pull herself together, but all that came out was, 'If I snored I'm going to die.' Her body arched into his despite herself. She stretched like a cat, right there in his arms. Lally stiffened with embarrassment and wished her emotions and responses would stop fritzing out on her.

Until Cam drew a deep, unsteady breath and went very, very still against her. 'You breathe like a kitten. You make purring sounds in your sleep. It's very…sexy.'

The words wrapped around her, made her feel desirable, gorgeous and lovely.

When had she stopped letting herself feel like that? Why had she stopped? The thoughts washed away as Lally registered the craving in his strong body, the desire mixed with gentleness in the fingers that stroked over her shoulder blades. They slowed as her body melted despite her, stroked to the back of her neck and oh, so softly drew her forward until his lips were a breath away from hers. 'May I?'

Kiss her? Love her? Do whatever he wanted with her and never, ever stop?

Her whispered, 'Yes,' ended in a sigh as his lips covered hers. Lally justified that it was only a kiss, one kiss, while rain fell on the roof above them. Cam tugged the sheet and blanket with his fist until it was wrapped around them, then she was snuggled hard against his chest while his mouth explored hers and their bodies pressed against each other.

There was always a point when the choice was made, a cut-off point, a chance to draw back; Lally and Cam pushed straight through that barrier with this one single kiss. He opened his mouth and offered her his tongue. She claimed him, exploring his mouth, letting their tongues brush, and to that claim she yielded herself.

'You're so beautiful.' Cam's hands skimmed over her upper arms. His fingers splayed over the side of her neck and speared into her hair. He buried his nose against her scalp, closed his eyes and inhaled, and his body tightened.

He pressed fully against her, tangled his legs with hers, and his muscles locked. 'I don't want to hurt you, Lally—emotionally. There are things I can't give you. In my past, I've proved that. This can't be…'

'I know.' And she did know. If Lally had

thought about anything, it was that neither of them wanted to get twisted up in something that they couldn't walk away from.

If her heart hurt a little at that thought, it was probably because she'd once had a lot more faith in her ability in relationships.

But that was then, and this was now, and she liked to think that she and Cam were friends; in some ways, wasn't that far steadier and more special than a lot of other things might be? If they both had histories that held them back emotionally now, well, maybe that meant this was okay for her with him: no false expectations, no surprises.

Just this. Now.

'I don't want it to be anything other than this.' Not more than right now; she didn't want the complication. Lally told herself this and tried not to notice the thoughts in the back of her mind that clamoured for so much more. 'We're just two people reaching for each other out of friendship and mutual desire. That's all it is. And it's allowed to be that.'

It was safe to take that, and to give it. It wasn't the same as thinking she'd fallen deeply in love, only to discover the man of her dreams had deceived her and that a marriage had failed as a result of their association.

She'd thought she was in love back then, but it had got a lot worse than even that marriage failure.

Cam searched her eyes in the dimness. She searched his too, though she didn't know what she was looking for and didn't know what he would find.

After a long moment, he stroked his fingers over her jaw.

Then she didn't think any more because he was kissing her with slow kisses and touching her oh, so gently.

Lally eased into those kisses and touches. She couldn't have said when they built to need, and when need became more need, until it consumed her and her emotions flared and rushed through her, even though she'd thought she knew what they were all about; now she didn't.

Sensation crowded through her too. Her mouth melted beneath his, yielded parts of her that she hadn't known were shut inside, hadn't imagined she would give to him because this shouldn't have been about that.

In a few short words, they'd laid down their rules. Tangled feelings, overwhelming feelings, were not part of this, yet she felt them pushing from inside to try to come out.

Lally could have panicked then but she didn't get a chance. Cam brushed her hair away from her face. Their clothes had disappeared; now he brought her to a place of desperate neediness. He eased her closer still and kissed her mouth.

Though he smiled and his eyes were calm, they were also full of heat, and his heart was thundering against her chest. His body quaked against hers and his fingers trembled as he stroked her face and slowly entered her. 'Lally.' His mouth closed over hers, worshipping her lips with the sweetest of kisses.

Lally's eyes fell slowly shut, and opened again as her body adjusted to his presence. How could she explain the sense of rightness, the feeling that their bodies had been made for each other, for this moment together? She looked into his eyes and didn't know why she needed this the way she did. How could she think about that question when all she could do was feel with her body, her senses and her emotions?

'Are you all right?' He kissed her lips. His body rested against hers, stilled within hers, as he waited for her answer.

'Yes.' She drew a breath. 'Yes.' And she was. Lally just knew that; she accepted it and let her worries go.

He loved her gently, loved her thoroughly, until every sense and nerve ending was tuned to him and only him. With whispered encouragement he helped her climb towards completion. His gaze locked with hers and he gave her all his pleasure and tenderness.

At the last moment he splayed his hand across her shoulder blades and pressed them heart to heart; he kissed her as she shattered in his arms, and he shattered with her.

When Lally thought it was over, he kissed her neck and shoulders, and used his hands to massage the muscles in her back, waist and over her hips until her body arched. He whispered her name and they made love a second time.

Dawn came and went as she lay in his arms, drifting between contentment, completion, half-consciousness and sleep. Thoughts didn't exist. How could they when all she could feel was the soft stroke of his fingers on her skin? When all she could hear was the even tenor of his breath against her ear? Lally let go and allowed herself to sleep once again.

Cam held Lally while she drifted on the edges of consciousness, and eventually as he gentled her with his touch she drifted all the way over and gave way to sleep. He kissed the top of her head and let himself tuck her close, then come to terms with feeling as though he held the most incredible treasure in his hands, treasure that he didn't want to let go of.

Had he done the wrong thing by her with this? When he'd woken with her in his arms, it had been too easy to reach for what he'd known deep down they both wanted.

But had that been best for her? And for him? Cam sighed and tucked a strand of her hair behind her ear. He pressed his lips to her temple and gave her the softest butterfly kiss. Where did all this tenderness in him for her come from? Cam hadn't been tender in his life like this. He hadn't wanted to wrap a woman up gently in his arms, hold her softly, cuddle her for as long as she needed, and then cuddle her some more because *he* needed it.

He didn't understand such feelings and he couldn't begin to imagine where he should try to go with them. There was no place he could go with them. Lally was his employee, his temporary housekeeper. Even that wasn't going to last. And Cam wouldn't last in an ongoing relationship with her, would never be able to settle, stick with it and focus on it, be committed to it.

He spent most of his time warring with his inability to sleep, filling his life and his world with way too much work to make the long hours pass. Yes, he'd slept in Lally's arms, but that wasn't normal for him. It had probably happened for some random reason, or because he'd become so totally exhausted that his body had finally allowed him to take that rest that he'd so desperately needed.

Cam knew his limits. He shouldn't have

allowed this to happen, but he had, and how would they deal with this now?

Cam sighed, forced himself to let her go, and then he climbed out of bed. He'd take a shower and get dressed, and maybe then he would think about all of this more clearly.

She'd said she didn't expect more than what they had shared. Cam had ended up feeling that they had shared a great deal more than he had expected. But exactly *what* had they shared? What made him feel this experience was different, deeper, so much more? And what did he do about any of that?

He had no answers.

CHAPTER THIRTEEN

'LALLY. About last night.'

'It was special; a gift. I'm choosing to see it as a gift and think of it as that.' Lally's rounded chin tipped up and her eyes glittered with determination.

She didn't quite meet Cam's eyes, not fully.

He couldn't blame her. Instead, he admired her so much for this show of strength when they both felt awkward and uncertain. Cam felt uncertain, and Lally *looked* uncertain beneath the façade of control and wilful good-cheer.

Cam should be thanking Lally for the gift. Nothing he'd experienced in his life had come close to what they'd shared last night. She'd brought him peace, sleep, rest and then the most moving intimacy he had ever experienced. 'I don't know what to say to you. It was—I've never; I can't explain.'

'You don't have to, Cam. You don't have to explain anything.' She kept her head facing forward.

They were in the convertible, headed for the first beach on their list for the day. A part of Cam had wanted to call the rest of their pebble-searching off and head straight back to Adelaide. But what would that solve? Nothing.

Yet Cam couldn't find the words to explain what was inside him. So he brought up one thing that should have been discussed last night— *before* they'd made love. 'Is there a chance you could end up…?'

'No.' She shook her head and warm heat flooded her face beneath the tan of her skin. 'I'm on the Pill—irregular periods.'

Right, well, that was good, then. No chance of a baby. Cam blew out a breath that had to be relief. He couldn't explain why the relief made his chest feel tight. His hands clenched around the steering wheel and he tried to relax them. 'Uh, this is the beach, just here.'

After stating the abundantly obvious, he pulled the car to a stop and they both climbed out.

It went like that all morning. They picked up pebbles, moved on to the next beach, picked up more pebbles. They were uncomfortable together, completely conscious of what had passed between them last night, silent about it, while unspoken further words screamed between them.

They finally finished finding pebbles and drove to the next town. They bought gourmet deli-sandwiches filled with prawns and other seafood on long rolls; they could eat them straight away, and they did, because it seemed the thing to do.

'We'll make good time back to Adelaide.' Lally got up from the park bench where they'd been sitting and brushed crumbs from her skirt.

Cam stood too, and his brow furrowed as he noted the shadows beneath her eyes. Those could have come from unhappiness or strain as easily as they could come from tiredness.

Lally stared at him as though willing him to just get them into the car so they could go. He returned her stare and dredged for words to say; he fought the need to hold her, and a wave of emotion rolled through him.

'Yes, we'll make good time,' Cam acknowledged, and Lally drew a shaky breath and headed for the car with such relief that he couldn't say another word. Not now. Not when she seemed so fragile.

And not when he didn't know what to say.

Cam just…didn't know.

'I'll let the supplier know we won't take the pavers, then.' Jordan, the site boss, shrugged his shoulders. 'My opinion stands. I'm sure the pebble mosaic will look great, and I'll help out with anything that's needed for it. But I think for the commercial plans you have for this place leaving the existing pavers down is going to make it look a little too comfy—like a big home, rather than a newly refurbished apartment-complex, albeit one created within an old building. Over all I don't think that's going to best serve the place.'

'And I respect your opinion, but I'll stick with the plans that I have for the mosaic and the existing paving of the courtyard area.' Cam shoved a hand through his hair. 'I have to go with my instinct on this. It feels right to do the area this way.'

Lally stood at Cam's side. It was afternoon. They'd arrived back, stepped out of the car and Jordan had asked for a few minutes to go over various matters. The courtyard area and a chance to get new pavers for it at a bargain price had topped the list.

Cam went on now. 'Lally's going to put in her mosaic, and you'll go ahead with the plans to get the garden surrounds into good order, but that's all that needs doing.'

'Okay. It's your call.'

The two men ended their discussion and the site boss walked away with no hard feelings.

That left Lally, Cam, a car full of pebbles, a few things that had been said and some that hadn't. Such as all the thoughts inside her head that Lally wasn't sure she wanted to examine. And the emotions that wrapped around the time she had spent in Cam's arms, how special that had been for her.

She wanted to walk away and never come back, to run and not stop running. At the same time, she wanted to step forward into Cam's arms, hold him, be held tight by him and never, ever let go. She hadn't been able to talk any more about it.

Lally had done what she'd promised herself she wouldn't do: she had let her feelings get involved. Now she had to un-involve them—somehow. She didn't know how.

Lally didn't know how she would get through the rest of her time with him at all. There were things inside her, deep, emotional things to do with them making love and the surrender to him that had somehow happened deep within her. Lally couldn't let herself think about those things, not if she wanted to get through this. Not with her past. With Cam, she'd taken something she had no right to. That was what kept coming to her.

'Lally.' Cam cleared his throat.

'There's nothing to say, Cam. Please, can we just forget it?'

'I'm not sure if I can forget.' He hesitated, then

said on a short burst, 'I fell asleep with you. I didn't believe I was capable of doing that. Maybe it was a one-off…' Doubt filled his words. 'I can't be settled. I'm a man who will never be able to stop in one place. I don't know how to be in a normal, loving relationship. I tried; I made a total wreck of it. And my mother…'

'It's not your fault that your mother can't settle down.' Lally did *not* believe that Cam was the same as his mother. 'And if you can't sleep, you can't sleep. Any person who knows you and love—*cares* about you, shouldn't ever feel anything about that other than empathy with your difficulties with that.'

Lally managed to stop her flow of words, but she couldn't stop what she'd almost said pouring through her heart. It rolled over her and consumed her.

She'd fallen in love with Cam. The knowledge was deep down inside her, true, total and absolute. She'd fallen for him before she'd ever made love with him, and of course she should have known that that was so.

Why else would she have needed that intimacy

so much, if not to put into expression what was inside her heart for him?

Oh, Lally. How could you fall in love with him? How can you protect yourself now that you've done that?

She had never felt this way about another person. Not Sam, and that shocked her, because she thought she'd loved Sam so much. Only Cam had said he'd tried to love once before and failed. That was his past, his secret—that he'd loved.

And don't expect him to love you, Lally. Don't expect it.

'I just want to do the mosaic for you.' For him, for her, to leave her mark here on this piece of property that would make a great family home, for a very large family to come and go. But not for Cam, who had almost no family and didn't want one of his own, and had only bought this place to develop it.

But he could be happy as part of a family. He wouldn't have to settle into one place to do that. If he needed to travel, couldn't he do that with someone at his side?

Oh yes, Lally? And would he choose you to be

that someone? A woman who broke up a marriage? Had an affair with a married man? Sent a woman into a care facility and her children into foster care?

Lally hadn't been able to do anything to help them. Sam should have done that but instead he'd walked away. Lally's thoughts put an end to any dream she might have had. She'd lost her right to dream, and all she could see that she had left to lean on in that moment was her professionalism. If she returned her focus to her work, maybe she would manage to get through this without Cam realising that she had discovered she loved him.

She didn't want him to know. It wouldn't change anything, would it? 'It shouldn't take me long to do the mosaic and have the water-feature put in. I'm happy to work with Jordan.'

'You're here for eight weeks.' Cam spoke as though he felt he needed to be assured of that.

It was her chance to say, no, the moment she finished the mosaic she would leave. Or turn around right now and walk away.

Lally couldn't do it.

She couldn't find it inside herself to lose any of the time she had left here, no matter what. Even though that probably made her a masochist. 'Yes. I'm here to take care of housekeeping duties, build the pebble mosaic and anything else that's required for your book research or your phone messages. You don't need to sacrifice time to help me with the mosaic. I'll be fine on my own.' She forced the words out. They had to be said. She would finish here, leave her gift, but that was all. 'It will be…better if I just do it.'

Cam's deep green gaze sought her eyes and locked. Oh, she wanted simply to let all the emotions inside herself loose, throw herself into his arms and hope for some miracle to make it all somehow work out.

But life wasn't that simple. Cam didn't want her with the kind of feelings she had for him, and if he did she'd have to explain her past—and Lally couldn't face seeing his reaction to that.

'Then I'll spend some time in my office now,' Cam said. 'Do some writing and catch up on my Sydney business interests.'

'That sounds like a good idea.' They'd had

one special night. They'd made love. Lally had fallen *in* love with her boss, but that didn't mean he'd suddenly developed the same feelings towards her. Nothing had changed between them other than there was now the awkwardness of knowing what they had shared.

Well, Lally could finish out her time here without letting that history or her current feelings get in the way of doing a good job as his employee.

She could. She *would!* 'I need to get working too. I want to prepare a good meal for tonight, as well as do some preliminary work on the mosaic.' No matter how hard she wanted to work on the mosaic, or how quickly she hoped to get it finished, she did have to make sure that taking care of her boss still came first.

Because Lally was the housekeeper, with a side order of helping him with his book research if required.

And Cameron was the boss. He was a little unconventional in his requirements at times, perhaps, because of his career as an author, but still the boss.

There couldn't be more between them. He hadn't offered more, and she needed to convince herself she didn't want or need more. Life had limits. In the case of 'Lally and Cam,' the limits were that there couldn't *be* a 'them' outside working together for a very temporary amount of time.

Lally wasn't sure she could lose that much, not yet. She didn't know how she would at all. So for the next five days she focused solely on doing her work on the mosaic and on looking after Cam. Her boss spent long hours in his office in the apartment, working. Sometimes at night she heard him out swimming laps in the pool. She swam, too, but never again at the same time as him.

Lally pushed her emotions down inside her and worked. And, despite doing that, or maybe because of it, the mosaic came together beautifully. When Lally stood back from the work on Friday night and dusted her hands down her legs over the denim cut-offs, she tried to give the mosaic an objective examination. Was it truly good? Or did she just want it to be, and so that was what she saw?

Lally admitted she not only wanted this work to be good, but she *needed* that, as her gift to Cameron. This was the part of herself that she could give to him and that he was prepared to keep. That was how Lally felt.

Oh, God. How could she walk away and leave him? Lally's heart filled with so much love for him in that moment that she hurt.

'It's brilliant.' Cam's quiet words sounded from a few steps behind her, deep words in the most gentle tone of voice, and then he was there. Lally had to do what she could to seem normal to him, while she felt her heart must truly be breaking in two, because she loved him so much. Yes, she could give him this, but she felt as though her one true opportunity to deeply give her love to him had been and gone too quickly.

Words rushed around inside her, came from her heart, filled her mind and had to be stopped before they crossed her tongue.

I don't want to leave you.

I don't know if I can stop loving you.

Can't there be a chance for us? Can't I be someone that you want enough that you overcome your hesitations about commitment? Can I hide my past from you, keep that secret and love you?

Of course that couldn't happen.

Oh, she hated this!

Lally turned slowly and tried simply to appear happy about his compliment, and about a job that he seemed to feel was well done. 'Thank you. I only finished it minutes ago. I was looking at it, trying to be objective. You're truly satisfied with it?'

His gaze shifted from the mosaic to her face. 'You've done an amazing job. You have true artistic talent, Lally. I think, if you wanted, you could do mosaics for a living.'

'Thank you.' Lally prayed that all her feelings weren't written across her face and tried to give him a simple, ordinary smile. If it was a little wobbly around its edges, she couldn't help that. 'I think the results work. The water feature is great; your site boss really came through with sourcing that.'

Cam's face relaxed into something close to a smile. 'He's a good site boss. I'd use him again any time. I didn't have the successful bid on the other property here in the city, but if anything else came up…'

'I imagine he'd be very happy to hear you'd use him again.' What if Cam told her that was enough now and let her go?

Suddenly Lally had her family on her mind. All the aunts, uncles, cousins, her sisters, brothers and parents. She'd missed them, and had worried, had wanted to get back to working with them. Yet now…

'It's a weird thing to ask, but I'm hoping I can talk you into going out for a fast-food meal instead of making dinner tonight.' He hesitated. 'You've worked really hard. We could go to a restaurant, of course, it's just—would you come out for a hamburger? If you're in the mood for that kind of food.'

'You don't have to reward me.' She didn't want him to feel that he needed to do that. 'I loved doing the mosaic. It made me happy to do that for you.'

Cam's face softened.

She wanted to believe it softened with love towards her, but he was just showing appreciation.

And yet, he pushed his hands into the pockets of his jeans and came close to shuffling his feet before he glanced up at her through the screen of his lashes. 'Will you come and eat salty junk-food with me—hamburger and fries? And maybe a completely nutrition-empty fizzy drink to go with them? Just…do that?' Not for a reward, just to do it.

'I will.' The words escaped her before she had any chance of recalling them.

Lally admitted she didn't want to take the words back.

If Cam wanted her company for an hour to go and eat fast food, she decided she would give herself that. There wouldn't be many more memories; maybe she should take them where she could find them.

'Good. That's good.' Cam took his hands out of his pockets and half-turned before he swung back to her. 'Half an hour? Time for you to shower off the dirt?'

'Yes.' She started towards their apartment.

His apartment, she corrected, in which she was a temporary, employed guest.

CHAPTER FOURTEEN

CAM stood in the centre of the living room, waiting for Lally. He didn't fully understand his edginess. No; that wasn't right. Cam knew the source of his inner upheaval. He'd been this way since he and Lally had returned from their trip to collect pebbles. He'd been edgy since they'd made love.

They'd both acknowledged they couldn't go there again, and Cam didn't need to know Lally's reasons for that. Yet in other things she was such an open girl. And Cam felt the need to understand her depths, even if his own weren't making a lot of sense to him right now.

Did he feel so affected by their love-making because it had followed *sleeping* beside her, sleeping whilst holding her? He'd never *slept* with a woman in his life. Sleep for him, solo, hadn't been a possibility for more than a certain amount of time. Sleeping with a *woman* in his bed? Yet with Lally he had slept, slept longer and better. He'd relaxed with her even in the face of wanting to make love to her.

Then he had made love to her. And now Cam had this urge to make sure she couldn't leave his employment, to find some way to keep her with him. Yet they couldn't remain lovers; it had been a mistake to let things go that way. If she stayed longer than the agreed time frame, was it even possible that they could relax into each other's company in a purely platonic way and be happy simply as boss and employee? As property developer–thriller writer and housekeeper?

Cam's mind told him that when the work on this complex was done—which would only be a few weeks away now—he had to let Lally go, say goodbye, move on with his life and forget her. That would be the smart thing to do.

So why ask her to go out to eat with him?

Because you've been here, and she's been here, and days have passed while you've both tried hard to get on with things, but you've missed her.

'I hope I didn't keep you waiting too long.'

Lally spoke in a carefully neutral tone from behind him.

He turned and took her in. For an hour or so there'd be nothing to do but concentrate on each other, and Cam wanted to concentrate on her, and somehow without putting them in a worse place than they were now. He resisted the urge to jam his hand through his hair. Did he truly know what he wanted about anything any more? 'I really do like you in red.' His voice deepened despite himself. 'It's vibrant. It suits you.'

She'd dressed casually in a black skirt with splashes of tiny red flowers over it. The skirt flowed to mid-calf and swirled about her legs when she walked; sandals left her feet beautifully revealed. Her hair was up in a pony-tail, she had gold, dangly earrings in her ears, and she wore a fire-engine red, clingy, sleeveless blouse that showed her slender curves to perfection and accentuated the long lines of her arms and the narrowness of her waist.

Cam's body noted all these things, but it was something a lot deeper than awareness that locked his eyes to hers and made it impossible to look away. Something that came from way deep down inside him and gave him pleasure to see her dressing in a way that allowed all of her vibrancy to shine out.

'You look beautiful.' The words escaped without his control.

Lally's face glowed beneath her tan and she dropped her gaze. 'Thank you. I bought the blouse at a stall at the market a few days ago; I guess it just caught my eye.' She seemed almost surprised by this, or perhaps a little discomfited.

'Bright colours suit you.' He'd told her so before, but this time her gaze rose to his and there were a thousand questions in her eyes.

But she only said, 'Thank you,' and suggested they get going.

Cam took his cue from her and hustled her to his car, and they drove the twenty minutes' drive to the restaurant. 'One of the workers mentioned this place and said the food's good, a cut above the ordinary.' Cam told her the name of the restaurant. Yes, he was making small-talk, but that was a start. If they could relax…

'I've heard of it, but I haven't been there. I

think it's a little more ritzy than an average fast-food outlet.' Lally seemed to be trying hard, too, and Cam hoped that she might want this time with him as much as he wanted it with her.

'So long as the food is salty, hot and at least a little bit fatty, I'll be happy.' He forced the words out and worked hard to produce a natural smile. 'There are just days—'

'When you want that kind of food.' Lally smiled a little, and then her smile became genuine.

Cam knew his had too.

Lally glanced again at Cam's face and some of her tension eased away. She didn't understand how she could relax in his company when her heart was aching so much. But she would rather be here with him than anywhere else in the world, and if she could have this, and they could enjoy themselves, well, she wanted it. She was glad he'd asked for this time.

Cam found a parking space and they walked the better part of a block to get to the restaurant.

The place was busy with a good cross-section of patrons; families, singles, people in business wear and tourists were all represented. Lally looked around and acknowledged she was happier in this moment than she'd been for days.

Just a little focused time with him, and she felt this way. Later she might feel twice as bad, but for now Lally was going to take what she could get.

A woman around Lally's age appeared and led them to a table tucked into a corner. She stared at Cam as they were seated, and then said, 'Oh, my God—aren't you Cameron Travers, the crime-thriller writer? I love your books. Oh, would you sign something for me?'

Cam signed the back of one of the paper menus for the woman and smiled her away. The back of his neck was red, and once they were alone he looked at Lally with a slightly trapped expression.

Delight washed through her, and she laughed. 'How often does that happen?'

'Not often, thankfully,' he growled. He lifted the other paper menu from the table and buried his nose in it. 'And we're short a menu now.' Cam lowered the one he held and laid it on the table so they could both look at it.

And, in the face of his discomfort at being recognised as a 'star', Lally relaxed the rest of the way into his company and just let herself enjoy their time together for what it was.

She was tired of trying to work things out in her head and heart. She loved this man with all her heart; that was fact. She couldn't avoid it or do anything about it, and there would be pain when she left him, but she wanted to try to enjoy her time with him until she had to leave. Was that so dangerous or foolish or silly? *Probably.*

They ordered the house special of a gourmet hamburger on a sour-dough bread roll baked on the premises and toasted to perfection, and a basket of fresh-cut chips. Lally gave up any pretence at being ladylike, picked up her hamburger in both hands and took a bite.

The tastes exploded on her tongue: the most divine, melt-in-your-mouth meat patty, crisp, fresh salad greens, spiced beetroot, succulent tomato, a barbecue sauce and mayonnaise that were both to die for. She watched Cam's face across the table as he, too, tried the hamburger.

His smile started in his beautiful green eyes and spread until it turned up the corners of his mouth. 'Do you think the trip was worth it?'

'Yes.' She'd have said so anyway for other reasons, but Lally simply smiled and went on, 'And we haven't even tried the chips yet.' She reached for the bowl in the centre of the table at the same time Cam did. Their fingers brushed, and his stilled where they touched hers.

He lifted his lashes and looked at her, and just for a brief moment his fingers stroked over hers before he took a chip, she took one too and they both ate.

'The, um, the chips are great too.' They were a perfect counter-balance for the delicious hamburger.

Cam reached for another one. 'The menu says they're oven baked, but they're so good I've decided to forgive the lack of excess fat.'

Lally licked the taste of salt from her lips and laughed, and a little silence fell as they paid attention to their food. It wasn't a bad silence but rather a comfortable one. Lally soaked it up with all her heart, studied each nuance of expression as it crossed his face and refused to think about any moment but right now.

The end of their meal coincided with the

people at the table beside theirs receiving their desserts. Lally cast one longing glance in that direction before she shook her head.

Her boss gestured to the menu. 'We can take a selection of desserts home for later, if you'd like?'

It was a small thing, but that thoughtfulness made Lally feel treasured. Or was it the soft expression in his eyes as he waited for her response? Oh, why couldn't they?

'I'm tempted, but I don't think I'll be able to eat a thing until tomorrow.' She pushed the thoughts away. 'Thanks for the offer, though.'

Cam settled their bill and minutes later they stepped out onto the busy street and strolled back towards his parked car.

He turned to her as they reached it. 'Thank you for doing that with me tonight.'

'Thank you for asking me to come along.' Lally sought for something light to say. 'Maybe you'll be able to use that in your book somehow too.'

Her boss thought for a moment. 'There are possibilities: the scent of fries leads my super sleuth to his answers…'

They were still laughing about it when Cam

unlocked the car. Lally stepped towards the kerb and glanced up as a woman's voice penetrated her thoughts.

'We'll go to look at the sports store, Danny. We just don't want to walk that far. Going in the car will be best.'

A man's voice joined in. 'I'll buy us all an ice cream after the sports store, so don't hassle your mum, okay?'

'Sorry, Mum.' A teenaged voice went on with a hint of cheeky cheerfulness, 'You know I love ya, even when I whinge.'

General laughter followed this comment.

Lally knew that female voice. It wasn't one she would ever be able to forget. Memories and guilt, so many things, hit her at once; at the depths of them was remorse. She didn't want to look, but she had to see. Her head turned, and her gaze shifted over the small group of people preparing to get into the car behind Cam's convertible.

The man looked about forty. There were three boys ranging in age; Lally didn't know the exact ages, but the youngest had been under two years old back then. They all looked a lot like Sam;

Lally noted that as she searched their young faces, searched all over each of them for signs.

And the woman was Julie Delahunty. Here. Right now. With all three of her sons. The group looked like a family, comfortable with each other. Happy.

In that moment, Julie looked up, recognised Lally, and her mouth pinched into a tight line while her face leached of every bit of colour. Her hands reached for the boys nearest to her, as though she needed to physically stop them from being taken from her side.

I am so sorry.

The thoughts were trapped inside Lally's mind, trapped deep in her heart. She'd written them to Julie long ago; her counsellor had helped her to get them sent to Julie at the care residence. There'd never been a reply; Lally hadn't expected one. But something in the expression on Julie's face now told her she'd received and read the words. So at least she did know of Lally's regret.

It doesn't change anything, Lally!

And it didn't.

Lally's hand rose, palm up, in a silent expression of supplication. Her mouth worked, though no words came out. Guilt and remorse ached in her heart.

Cam's voice impinged. 'Lally? Sweetheart? What is it?'

She felt the touch of his hand on her arm, his fingers closing around her wrist in a gentle clasp as his body turned to hers, as though he would shield her from whatever harm was trying to befall her.

In all that had happened between Lally and Cam, she'd managed to push this part of her history mostly away. She hadn't let herself look at this, admit this, acknowledge how it stood between her and certain possibilities in life. Happiness; she didn't deserve happiness. Lally didn't see how that could ever change.

The woman hustled her sons into the car. The man spoke to her in a low voice, glanced in Lally's direction, and his mouth tightened too.

Lally wanted to turn, hide her face in Cam's chest and just will it all away. Shame stopped that thought before it fully formed. Lally had longed to be able to love Cam and have him love her back—oh, she admitted this—but how could she ever have hoped for that?

If Cam knew.

The family drove off into traffic. At least they were gone. There were other impressions from these moments trying to register, but Lally couldn't see past Julie's stricken face, her hands reaching for her sons.

Lally let Cam put her into the passenger seat and they too headed into traffic in the other direction, heading for…

Not home. Heading for Cam's property development.

'Who were they, Lally?' Cam's words were stern in a way she'd never heard from him before. 'It's clear that seeing those people has hugely upset you. I want—I *need* to know why. If you're in trouble, I'll help you, protect you.'

'Her name is Julie Delahunty.' Lally did not want to speak of this, but she couldn't leave Cam worrying for her sake.

She would tell him the same part of this that she had told her family. Lally's voice was a flat monotone as she said, 'I had an affair with her husband six years ago. Julie's three sons were smaller then, still very dependent on their parents, obviously.'

Dependent. 'When Julie found out about the affair and became…unwell over it, Sam, he walked away. He didn't care about her or his sons.' Sam hadn't cared about Lally, either, but that paled in comparison. Lally clamped her lips together. She'd already said more than she had wanted to.

She'd put the words to Cam more revealingly than the cold, minimal facts she had told her family six years ago.

Cam's hands remained relaxed on the steering wheel and his gaze was clear and steady as he cast a quick glance her way before turning his attention back to the road.

Lally saw his compassion, but he took care not to show pity or judgement.

He asked quietly, 'And the gentlemen with her just now wasn't her husband?'

'No. I don't know who he was.' Lally dredged her mind for a way to end this conversation. 'Please, Cam.'

What did he think of her, now that he knew she'd had an affair?

It didn't matter to Lally. There was no hope for her with him. This had just underlined that fact for her. The rest was irrelevant.

'I love my family.' The words were jerky; they exposed her, came out as long-buried guilt and pain forced their way past her control and reserve. Past six years of silence. 'I've been trying—'

'Ever since to make it up to them?'

Somehow they were inside the apartment, and with the door closed behind them Cam threw his car keys onto the entry table and led her to sit on the sofa in the living room. He clasped her hand in his. Lally didn't deserve his comfort but they were here and he wasn't letting go.

She wanted to run, but a part of her wanted to confess things she'd not confessed, except to that counsellor who hadn't been able to accept, or judge, or punish, or forgive, who had only been able to acknowledge and try to guide Lally so she could fix this for herself.

Fix a guilt and heartbreak that was unfixable. So Lally had buried it deep, and, yes, she had hidden out in her family. She had needed to feel safe.

'Won't you tell me? Maybe I can help somehow.' Cam looked into Lally's beautiful brown eyes, and thoughts and emotions he'd stifled in the days since he'd made love to her bubbled to the surface inside him. 'You've done so much to try to help me.'

This beautiful girl had been punishing herself for so long. That was so clear now. He had half known, had half guessed that already from her silent determination not to get involved with him. He'd guessed it was because of a man somehow, but he hadn't guessed all this guilt.

She'd punished herself by wearing dull coloured clothes. She'd sown herself into serving her family and hadn't wanted to step outside of working among them. Lally had hidden herself because of guilt.

Within her family, she had maybe even tried to work off what she perceived as her sin by giving, giving and giving to them. Was Lally seeing her past in a genuine light? Or was it coloured, *mis-*

coloured, by a young girl's memories and guilt that had never been resolved?

'How old are you now, Lally?' He asked the question in a calm tone while his fingers stroked over the back of her hand.

She'd relaxed that hand into his clasp, though he wasn't sure if she realised she had done that, trusting him with that much of herself. Cam wanted to help her, but he also wanted her to trust him with so much more. The thought drew his eyebrows together but he didn't get a chance to examine it before Lally answered his question.

'I'm twenty-four.' Her brown eyes shimmered with regrets and hurt. 'It was in my CV.'

'Yes. So you're twenty-four now.' Cam pressed on, 'That means you were eighteen when you were seeing that woman's husband—Julie, was it? And how old was he?'

'He was ten years older.' Lally bit her lip. 'I knew it wasn't a good idea to see someone that much older.'

A part of Cam wanted to go and find the other man and make *him* take responsibility for hurting the young girl Lally must have been then. He bit back that impulse and went on, 'Did you know he was married?'

Brown eyes met his gaze. 'No. I didn't know he was married.' She bit her lip.

And Cam said softly, 'What happened?'

She drew a deep breath and the words slowly came out. 'He swept me off my feet. He flattered me, said he loved the way I dressed in my bright colours, loved my vibrancy. Sometimes, when I've thought about it…' She stopped and swallowed hard, shook her head.

'You were very young, and you were preyed on by a man who must have known better.'

That's not your fault, Lally. Let yourself accept these facts and find the forgiveness you've been dodging all this time.

Lally's fingers gripped his as she went on. 'My family said it wasn't my fault. But they didn't know—I talked to a counsellor after it happened. I didn't need to say more to the family. It wasn't necessary.' Lally fell abruptly silent.

'It wasn't your fault, Lally.' He squeezed her hand. 'I'm guessing you've blamed yourself, perhaps, for his marriage breaking down?' It wasn't hard to work that out. 'You shouldn't. It was *his* behaviour that caused the breakdown of his marriage.'

'You don't understand.' Lally shook her head. Her tone became tortured. 'When she found out, his wife had a breakdown. Sam just walked away from all of it. Julie got put into a care facility and her sons were placed into foster care.'

She drew a shaky breath. 'I couldn't help. I broke up an entire family, harmed innocent children, made Julie so unhappy that she lost her grip on…'

And there it was; all of Lally's guilt was finally out there. Cam felt absolutely ferocious in that moment, ferocious in his need to protect her, to reverse time, to take this pain away for her. He needed to heal her as she had tried so hard to help him heal his insomnia, and help him in so many other ways.

Tenderness welled up with that protectiveness, soft emotions he couldn't name but had to act on.

'She was with her sons today,' he said carefully. 'That looked like a permanent arrangement. They looked like well-adjusted, typical boys for their ages, and she looked happy in her role as their mother, with a man who appeared to be her current partner.'

'Yes.' Lally frowned. 'She looked well and happy…at least, until she noticed me.'

'You can't change the past.' Cam said it in acknowledgement. 'But you're not to blame for it, Lally. So be glad that you saw her today, that you know she is well now and has her children with her. Let it go now so you can move on with your life.'

Lally searched Cam's eyes and couldn't believe that she had told him all of this. She felt lighter, somehow. Not suddenly all better, but Cam had accepted it. He hadn't judged her. 'How can you not think badly of me?' That was what Lally couldn't understand. She was happy that Julie's life seemed better now, but that still didn't change the past.

And, whatever Cam thought about this, it didn't change the fact that he didn't *love* her. He was kind, thoughtful, accepting. But he didn't love her. So what had changed, really?

'I need to get an early night.' Lally hit the end

of her ability to cope, to think. To do anything. She just needed to get away. 'Thank—thank you for tonight, for the meal and for…this. But will you excuse me?'

Somehow she was on her feet and her hand was back in her possession, and Lally didn't wait to see what would happen after that. There was nothing that could happen. Because she and Cam didn't exist. They just didn't, and that was that.

CHAPTER FIFTEEN

'THANK you again for meeting me here. I realise I'm stepping over a line, but I hope you can understand why. You need to talk to your daughter, help her get this out so she can stop punishing herself.' Cameron's voice came to Lally clearly as she stepped around a corner stall at the market.

Two days had passed since they'd come across Sam's ex-wife and her new family, since Lally had admitted her guilt to Cam. She'd been silent, withdrawn, thinking about his words. But what difference did it make in the end?

'I should have guessed there might be more to this.' Mum's voice choked up. 'I feel just awful. We all thought Lally just needed a little push to get her to trust in life again, so we pretended no one needed her help right now.' Mum drew a sharp breath. 'All we did was take away the sense of safety that she needed. When that affair happened, we wished we'd understood things sooner so we could have protected her from Sam Delahunty. We all felt we'd let her down. We didn't know about…the rest.'

Shock drove Lally forward. She stepped into their path. There was Cam, and there was Mum; Mum saw her and handed a bag of something to Cam. Lally was in Mum's arms, throttling back emotion because she didn't want to cry in front of him.

'Oh, Lally, I'm so sorry.' Mum's touch went straight into Lally's heart to wrap around a part of her that she hadn't realised was so broken. It didn't matter then that Cam appeared to have sought Mum out, or that they'd been discussing personal things about her.

Lally buried her face in Mum's neck and breathed in deep, and they stayed like that for a long minute.

Finally Mum stepped back and held her at arm's length so she could look deep into her eyes, brown eyes to brown eyes, filled with so much love. 'I should have talked to you about it more, Lally. I didn't realise…'

'I shouldn't have held onto the guilt the way I did.' Lally finally accepted that now. She hadn't meant any of Julie's hurt or the hurt of her sons. She had been tricked and she had made mistakes, but she hadn't done anything out of malice, lack of care or anything else like that. She could never have guessed what would happen.

'I can't regret that I spoke about this, Lally.' Cam's words were low and careful. 'I thought your mother needed to know.'

And she did. Lally's gaze shifted from Mum's face to Cam's, where he stood silently beside them.

Cam gripped the bag Mum had given him in tight fingers and used his other hand to rub at the back of his neck. 'Me meeting your Mum this morning—I got her phone number out of the book. She brought painting materials. One of your aunts is being pushy about you painting again, apparently.'

He shook his head. 'What am I talking

about? That can wait.' Cam seemed at a loss as to how to go on.

Lally's heart melted all over the place because, whatever else there was, his care was so clear.

Lally looked deep into Cam's eyes and he looked just as deeply back. How did she respond to his kindness, to this thing he had done for her sake? How did she deal with all the feelings and emotions whirling about inside her right now? Feelings about Sam, Julie and the three boys, yes—but even more deeply about Cameron. Somehow, it was a big tangle. Lally had to figure out how to unravel it, if she could, or perhaps how to weave it together within herself. To weave her past in, and let it be part of her, but the right kind of part.

That wouldn't make a difference with Cameron; of course it couldn't. He didn't love her the way she loved him. He was wonderful and special, but she mustn't kid herself that his kindness meant he had very special feelings towards her.

But if she could convince him that he could commit? That his insomnia didn't need to get in the way of a relationship for him? That his past failure in a relationship didn't have to mean his next attempt would fail, that he, too, could address his past? That it was okay to acknowledge that his mother hadn't cared well for him and he wasn't obliged to feel close to her? If only Lally could help Cam see all his value purely for who he was. What was she thinking? None of it made any difference to *her* limitations.

'Lally, darling.' Mum touched her arm gently and released her. 'We do need to talk, but I'm guessing maybe that needs to wait a little.' Though she didn't glance in Cam's direction, Mum's eyes were full of far too much understanding, *Love* and understanding, that had always been there.

Mum started to turn away, and Lally uttered, 'We *will* talk, Mum. I'd like that. And I want to be taught painting.'

'I'm so glad, Lally. It's your tradition. It will be good for you to try it. I love you, Lally.' Emotion filled Mum's face. She gave a nod and a wobbly smile and disappeared, and Lally turned back to Cam. There were a thousand things she wanted to say; Lally couldn't find the words for any of them, and she said lamely, 'I saw your note that said you'd come to the market and would take care of the shopping.'

Lally had come to join him on the very thin pretext of helping. Even though she'd been withdrawn and hadn't wanted to talk about her past any further with him for the last couple of days, she had longed to be close to him, just *be* with him, in his company. Or something.

'I took care of the shopping.' He indicated the bag at his feet, and as he did so placed the bag her mother had handed to him inside it as well. 'Are you angry, Lally?' His gaze searched hers. 'That I interfered? After we talked, I…didn't feel that I'd fully helped you to let go of all that blame you'd been carrying. I thought maybe your mother could.'

Cam searched Lally's dear face as he waited for her answer, and he finally understood.

He had fallen in love with Lally. It was so simple, really; he didn't know how he could have missed it. He couldn't miss it now because it consumed him. He had a need that was all about her, all about needing to love her, care for her, help her resolve her problems and hurts, be there for her, protect her, encourage her.

Where could he go with these feelings?

'I'm not upset, not really. You wanted to help me.' Lally started to turn. In a moment she'd walk back to the property development.

'Please.' Cam didn't want to lose these quiet moments with her, not yet. He didn't know what he wanted to do, or say... 'Would you come to the park with me? It's not far from here, not far out of our way.'

'I guess that would be okay.' Lally didn't understand Cam's motivation.

She should give him her resignation and leave before this got any more complicated.

The smart, sensible, take-care-of-yourself part of her suggested that would be the thing to do.

But Lally had been running and backing away and not addressing things for long enough. If Cam wanted to go to the park, they would go to the park.

She walked silently at his side until they entered the park. Cam kept walking and Lally wondered if he would ever speak, and if he did what he would want to say. Lally had things to say. 'You said you'd had a failed relationship—in your past. That sounds as though *you* feel to blame for *that.*'

'I did. I'll explain.' Cam took Lally to the makeshift jetty. There was no little boat this morning, just the lake and quietness. He set down the bag. He'd taken the time during their walk here to try to marshal his thoughts into some kind of order; he wasn't sure if he'd achieved that. 'I'll come back to that.'

All he knew was he needed to express these feelings that were inside him. He needed Lally so much that he couldn't make himself step aside, not if there was any chance that they could find a way.

'I remember you interviewing me on the water. I was nervous that morning.'

'I'm nervous now.' He held her arm while she sat on the edge of the jetty. The jetty stuck out far enough over the water at the end that they could sit without their feet touching the water. Cam sat beside her and turned to face her. So much love welled up inside him. He didn't know what to do with all the feelings.

'Why would you be nervous?' Lally asked and shook her head. 'I'm the one with the horrible past and six years of going around with my head in the sand not dealing with it. I'm glad Mum knows it all now. Somehow that's a weight off my mind. I didn't want to hide it from my family, but I did, and then it felt too hard to try to tell them.'

Lally loved him for his admission of nerves. 'When I talk to Mum, maybe she might be able to help me work out a…healing process.' She dipped her head before she forced it up again. 'You might think it's silly, but there are spiritual things Mum could help me do.'

'I think that's a great idea.' Cam didn't even blink, simply gave his support.

Her expression softened as she searched his gaze. '*Your* mother might be still on the face of the earth, but she doesn't keep contact and closeness with you the way she should. I'm sorry you've missed out on that all your life.'

'You said something a while back about us

moving around so much that I must have not known where I'd wake up half the time.' Cam had pushed the comment aside at the time. Maybe it had been easier to go on blaming his insomnia just being how it was.

'It's so long ago, but I developed a fear of sleeping back then. I used to be afraid that I'd wake up and Mum would have abandoned me somewhere and gone on without me.' He shook his head. 'It sounds stupid now. I've been a grown man and in charge of myself for a long time. I never thought about it until after that night that I…slept with you.'

'You trained yourself into a habit of not sleeping, and until you figured that out about yourself…'

'I had no hope at all of sleeping and feeling relaxed unless I felt deeply happy and secure.' As he had felt the night he'd held Lally in his arms and had drifted to sleep to the kittenlike sounds she'd made while she slept. Was it any wonder he'd woken and needed to express all his feelings to her the way he had? 'You gave me that feeling, and so much more.'

The sleep didn't even matter, and Cam needed

to tell her that. 'I'm not doing a very good job of expressing myself. I don't need to get some instant or fabulous fix for my sleep issues. If I can go back for some further professional guidance about that, get in a better place with that now that I've realised that childhood fears have most likely contributed to the problem, that will be great—but if not...'

He drew a breath. 'I don't think I have to let that issue, or the hours that I work, or the way I was raised and my lack of closeness with my mother, stop me from trying to make a success of a relationship that matters to me.' He swallowed. 'Where there's a deep enough love, can't most things be figured out?'

He searched her eyes, and he wasn't sure what he saw there. Was it kindness that made her eyes shine in that way? Cam wanted her to let him in to her heart.

He took Lally's hands in his and gently squeezed her fingers. 'I thought I couldn't be in a relationship. I blamed that on the insomnia, my workaholic tendencies. What would I have to offer a woman? That's what I asked myself. I failed once, but I've realised now that I didn't love Gillian.' He drew a breath. 'I doubt she really loved me.' That didn't matter anyway, now.

'I've fallen in love with you, Lally. You're so deep in my heart and I can't bear the thought of you leaving me. I'd been wracking my brains for ways to keep you with me. I thought of asking you to be my travelling housekeeper, to go everywhere with me. But I don't want only that. I want *all* of you.' That was Cam's admission, and what he needed to say.

'I don't understand.' Lally wanted to comprehend this—her heart begged for that—but how? 'You know about my past.'

'And you know about mine. I want a chance for both of us to reach out and be happy. Past histories—they are *in* the past, Lally. They can make us stronger and better. They don't have to hold us down or hold us back.'

Cam had realised this; he needed Lally to see it too.

Lally looked at Cam. He wanted her to be happy with him? He'd said he loved her? Lally took the wondrous thought deep inside herself.

Could it be true? It could, because Cam wouldn't say that if he didn't mean it.

The knowledge finally penetrated all the way to Lally's heart. Hope rose there. She looked into Cam's eyes and knew she had to fully open her heart. 'I'm in love with you too. It happened the night we made love. I didn't understand then, but I realised later, and I didn't know how to deal with my feelings. I was certain you wouldn't be able to feel the same way towards me.'

'You love me?' Cam uttered, and his hands tightened, one around her hand, the other over her shoulder. The next moment she was snatched against his chest and his arms were against her back, his hands pressing into her shoulder blades before he reached very, very gently and raised her face so he could look into her eyes. 'Say that again.'

'I love you.' Lally did, and it felt so good to admit it and to realise that he loved her too.

'Do you truly believe we can have a future?' Dared she ask?

But, yes, Lally did dare ask because she longed for, wanted and *needed* a future with Cam. If there was any chance of that, she wanted to grasp it. For the first time in six years, she felt hope.

'Yes. Yes, Lally,' he uttered in the deepest, most sincere voice Lally had ever heard. 'I want for ever with you, and we can have it if we both try.'

Lally slowly nodded. 'If we love and accept. I would understand about your wakefulness, Cam, even if it never got any better. And your need to focus on your writing while your muse is willing to talk.'

Cam laughed and shook his head. 'I still have a deadline, but I must admit writing hasn't been my first priority since the night we made love. I've kept working, but all I've really wanted to think about is you.'

He drew a breath. 'Because that old relationship fell apart, and Gillian said she couldn't cope with my work focus and sleeplessness, I thought I didn't have enough to give. And I'm *not* close to Mum. You have a big family. I don't know if I could fit in.'

Lally searched Cam's face once more and knew his concerns were genuine. She smiled gently. 'You seem to get along okay with Mum.'

He nodded. 'Your mother is a kind, giving, lovely person…just like you.'

Oh, his words went straight to Lally's heart and found their way deep inside it. She let a teasing edge touch her smile as she responded, 'So just multiply Mum by about a hundred and you have my family. Since you're a rather great person to get along with yourself, I think you would be fine fitting in.'

It hit her then just how deep this conversation had gone. They were talking about 'for ever' kinds of things. Did Cam want…?

'I'd like to be part of your big family.' Cam's expression sobered into a deep, open love, into hope and need. 'And I would like to have babies with you, make our own special family, when we're ready for that step.'

In that moment, Lally gave herself utterly to this man who had been her boss, her lover, a friend and would now become everything to her. The thought of having his child overwhelmed her, filled her heart with a love she couldn't begin to comprehend.

Lally buried her face against Cam's chest and

let her fingers rest over his heart. The brush of his mouth against her forehead made her lift her face, and he kissed her lips softly and drew back to look into her eyes.

'Will you marry me, Lally? Let me hold you in my arms at night, love you, be with you whether I sleep at your side or stay awake, and be happy because I'm with you?' He hesitated. 'I don't know if I can settle in one place. It's not something I've tried, but this property development—I thought from the day I met you that it would make a good family home, so maybe we could try…'

'Yes.' Yes to all of it, including trying. 'We can work those things out. We'll both need to adapt and understand what we want out of life together.' Lally would go anywhere with him. In her heart, she knew that, though it would be nice to be close to her family when possible.

'I won't take you from them, Lally.' He said it gently and she knew he'd read her emotions on her face.

Lally was just fine with Cam knowing her feelings so well. 'If we travel, we can still come home here to the family, if you don't need to be based in Sydney for your business.'

'I've become quite adroit at running that business from afar. There's no reason why I can't continue to do so.' Cam smiled and hugged her. 'I will love your family, but I'll love you most of all. We can have this, Lally. We can go forward.'

She nodded. 'Let our pasts be what have formed us to this point, but we'll form our futures with each other.'

'Yes.' Cam's voice deepened. 'Yes, Lally.'

And there, on a makeshift jetty at the edge of a small lake in a suburban park, Cam proceeded to tell Lally about all the hope that was in his heart for their 'for ever.'

And Lally soaked up every word while the sun rose over the lake and sent vibrant sparkles of colour shining through the mist.

After a long moment, Cam said, 'I can't wait to marry you, to see you walk towards me on that special day and know you're going to be truly and completely mine to love and care for always.'

'Oh, I can't wait for that either.' Lally's heart filled with love for him.

His arms closed about her, and he turned her face up and kissed her mouth gently. 'Our future starts right now. I want you in all of my life, Lally. Everything. I want you to learn to paint from your mother, or whoever else in your family will teach you. And I want to encourage you with more mosaic work.'

Lally's heart filled all over again with love for this wonderful man. 'We can travel all over Australia for a while leaving a trail of property developments with pebble mosaics in their courtyards if we want to.'

Cam's gaze met hers, with all his heart right there for her to see. 'So long as we keep coming home to *this* property, and settle here eventually. There'll be room for visits from all your relatives, and my mum, if I can ever convince her to stop by.'

'Maybe one day we will convince her.' In this moment, Lally believed that anything might be possible.

Home, happiness, family and a future. And, though they did travel, that was exactly how it turned out to be.